THE REUNION

M.D. NEU

Published by Water Dragon Publishing
waterdragonpublishing.com

Experience our other Dragon Gems titles
waterdragonpublishing.com/dragon-gems

ISBN 978-1-969655-10-4 (Trade Paperback)

10 9 8 7 6 5 4 3 2 1

For my husband, my family and my friends.
I love you all.

ACKNOWLEDGEMENTS

A SPECIAL THANK YOU to CJ, Nick, Lisa, Joe, without whom none of these characters would have come to life. You guys helped me to find my voice and gave me a place to write and tell stories.

Thank you and much appreciation to Barbara, Randall, Jeanne, Arlo, Bud, Robert, Jim and Isabel providing the encouragement to get this story out there. And a special thanks to my editor, Jason, who pushed me to make this the amazing story it is.

THE REUNION

1

T EDDY STOOD ATOP THE GRASSY KNOLL, glancing down at Lakeview. *Has it really been twenty years?* The smell of fresh roses and lilies filled his senses. From there, he could see all of the town, Main Street, the radio tower, the old CAGE manufacturing building, the hospital, the school, even the country club. But most importantly, he could see the lake. He sighed, supposing that was something that would never change. The town was still all there—barely.

He peeked over his shoulder to where the town sign had once stood. All that remained was busted-up bricks and some aged wood with faded paint. He could barely read the name and town motto:

Lakeview
Set your spirit free

Teddy frowned and shook his head. "Yeah, right." He sighed.

He reached into his pocket and pulled out a small anxiety pill and popped it into his mouth and dry swallowed it. *Anyway, those that got out are coming back. Still, it brings up so much pain and hurt.* He glanced back at the ruined sign. "It wasn't all bad, of course. There were good parts." A soft chuckle escaped him. Teddy remembered the day that led up to his return home so many years before. His mother had just passed away, and he and Lane were about to split for the last time.

"That was a long time ago." Teddy wiped at his eyes and cleared his throat, thinking of Lane and that final fight. Having to go, leaving Nick was the worst, but he was relieved to be away from Lane and his bullshit. In a way, he was able to escape from that cage too. Still, Nicky had been just a boy and had no idea what was happening. The more he thought about it, the more his heart began to pound and all the old ghosts came to light. Every year, when he came back to Lakeview, was the same story. Standing here, looking down at the town, it was like it was happening all over again.

A gust of wind ruffled the leaves on the road. The clouds always seemed to surround the town this time of year. He rubbed his arms and hurried back to his Mustang. He reached into the car, pulled out his jacket, and slipped it on. Somehow, it didn't warm him, but it kept the strengthening breeze off his back and arms. He patted the pocket. Not finding what he was looking for, he glanced back to the car. On the passenger seat was his pill bottle. He leaned down and nabbed it, then put it in his pocket.

I'm probably going to need these today.

A rumble of thunder rolled off in the distance, near the far end of the lake. He scanned the town again. He couldn't see his old house anymore. Over the last few years, it had vanished more and more. He supposed if he drove by it, assuming he could remember where it was, there would be nothing left.

So many mistakes. If I'd believed him, then none of this would've happened. He shook his head. "It's all so crazy, but it happened. No wonder no one ever believed me or the others."

There was another clap of thunder as he pictured the day he'd come back to town. It was six years before everything went to shit. When he was young, he had felt like this town was a cage, but it ended up being his freedom when he returned after Lane. *Maybe some prisons can never be escaped no matter what we try or how hard we want it.* A smile bloomed across his lips at the memory of driving down the main street in full drag, big hair, and a brand-new pink Mustang.

My god, those people had no idea what to do, or what they were in for. He groaned at the thought of his behavior when he'd showed up.

Teddy shook off his trek down memory lane as he pulled up to what had once been the heart of the towns main street. He applied the brakes not bothering to pull into a parking space, Teddy turned off the ignition of his classic Mustang, the thrum of the engine falling silent.

The road before him was empty, like all of the town. He opened the door and hefted himself out as damp cold air bit the back of his neck and ears, his jacket offering no protection.

Like the streets, the buildings were in complete

disrepair—most, if not all, were shells of their former selves. Not even the boarded-up windows and doors were left in place.

Things are so different.

He adjusted his jacket collar trying to protect his neck from the cold. The government named it an *incident*, but Teddy called it a *disaster*. He fussed with his keys and slipped them in his jacket pocket and studied his dilapidated surroundings. No one cared anymore, and no one talked about what happened. Twenty years wasn't long in the grand scheme of the universe, but it was long enough for people who wanted to forget.

He took a deep breath and could taste the coming storm. Soon enough, it would rain.

He continued to take in the ruined storefronts. Life once hummed up and down this street, but after CAGE Manufacturing burned down in a freak fire and didn't reopen, there wasn't anything left to keep the town going. Like so many small towns with nothing more to offer, Lakeview died.

The sign from his old hair salon swung in the gusting wind. Ultimately, it would fall to the crumbling sidewalk and be forgotten, just like everything else. He frowned. No one would ever buy the building he still owned. Holding the deed to the structure was only a minor annoyance and ultimately would mean nothing, even to him.

A flash of lightning off in the distance caught his eye when he turned back to his salon. Doc stood there lifeless and pale. He was holding Jenny's hand. Doc removed his hat, revealing a bullet hole through his temple. Jenny was no longer recognizable, her blond hair thick with blood and her pretty face carved up like spoiled hamburger.

"Not real." Teddy shook his head and the images vanished.

He turned and there in front of him stood Kasandra, blood dripping from her mouth. All her teeth were gone, and there was a huge gash along the side of her face dripping with blood and gore.

"It's me, Miss Thing. Can you make me look human again?"

Teddy stumbled back. His heart banged in his chest. He closed his eyes, then opened them again. The nightmare image was no more.

Teddy swiped the sweat from his brow, then kicked at a rock near his foot.

Why do I keep coming back?

Perhaps it was the ghosts from so long ago. To see those that understood the loss and the shared pain. Maybe it was time for a final goodbye. It could be for answers he would never get. Towns like Lakeview never revealed all their secrets. But something had forced him back, year after year. Something pulled them all back.

As the clouds darkened around the town, he found himself outside the old CAGE building. He ran a hand over the blood-stained road. The air was still thick with a coppery scent.

"This is where the end began." A shiver ran down his spine as he stood.

Teddy followed the road back up Main Street as he toured the remains. He strolled to the empty diner. A smile grew across his lips. He had so many good memories of Casey and Lisa eating, harassing Greg about his drunk karaoke rendition of "Love Shack." No matter how bad, Greg managed to get everyone up on their feet.

He shook his head, a sigh escaping his chilled lips.

A flash of lightning grabbed his attention and when he glanced back into the diner, he saw Casey, Lisa, and Greg standing at the window. Casey had cuts all over her face, a large piece of glass embedded in her left eye socket. The right side of Lisa's face was gone, the part remaining was blackened and ragged. There was a large hole where Greg's face should have been, through which he could see Dee standing there with a blank cold gaze.

Teddy gasped and stepped back. The smell of rot and decay assaulted his senses. "You're not real. That didn't happen." He closed his eyes. "It's just my anxiety. I'm going to see you all in a little while, and you'll be just fine."

An old newspaper gathered at Teddy's feet. He glimpsed the heading, "Local Teen goes on Murderous Rampage as Citizen's Riot, Town in Shambles!", before a strong gust of wind caught the paper and blew it off down the street.

To listen to the rumors and speculation, you would have thought the whole town had lost its mind. But it was only a few important people, people who could control the town and the news. *If I only believed him, none of this would have happened.* It amazed him how one small group could effect such devastation and pain on so many. They would have a penance to pay, of that he was certain. Teddy checked the door handle as he continued to relive that night, that awful night, when everything changed.

The meteor shower. Nick. My car. All that blood.

He pushed the awful images from his mind that wasn't why he was here. He peered through the diner's dusty, smashed window. The broken tables and chairs, the shattered refrigerator case. The shredded booths. More memories rushed back to him. He and Casey sitting at the booth in back. Casey preparing her playlist for the radio station between bites of toast. They were laughing. Dee ran around, attending to customers, while Bill was in back, cooking. Casey looked out the window, right toward him, their gazes meeting.

There was a flash of lightning, and Dee and Bill were standing at the window, their cold dead eyes focused down the street toward the old CAGE building. They turned to Teddy and pointed. Nick stood off in the corner alone and shaking. He met Teddy's gaze and held up his blood-covered hands. Teddy shook his head and turned away only to come face to face with Casey, her face pale, the cuts and glass reappeared. Her hair was again a clumped bloody mess, her only eye hollow and lifeless.

"That's not Casey, and that isn't Nick." Teddy forced his eyes closed and reached for his pills. He fumbled with the lid before quickly taking another pill. When he opened his eyes, Casey smiled stunnngly and her flowing brown hair caught what little light there was.

"Beautiful."

If only she were a guy. Teddy chuckled at the thought. *Like that would make a difference.*

Casey wasn't the same after the disaster. None of them were. How could they be? But she took it the hardest, blaming herself for not getting an emergency broadcast out fast enough. It wouldn't have mattered; by the time he and the others figured out what was happening, it was too late.

Teddy made his way back to his Mustang. The car was no longer bright pink as it had been in days long gone by.

It was now a sleek black. It wasn't as flashy or as outrageous as he once liked, but it was still fun to drive.

After starting the engine, he screeched down the road to CAGE. This time, instead of an empty burned-out shell of a building, a crowd of people stood outside the structure as it once had been. He slowed to a stop as a car sped past and into the crowd. One body flew through the air and hit the pavement with a wet crunch in the same spot he'd seen the bloodstain earlier. The bystanders all turned and faced him, their empty faces all focused on him. Watching him. Judging him. No reaction to the tragedy that they just witnessed.

Teddy shook away the image and focused on the street in front of him. "It's not real; none of it is real. Everyone is fine. My meds need to kick in, so I won't see that anymore." He continued down Main Street away from the ghostly images. The once pristine lawns and trees were now nothing but overgrown weeds and dead stumps. He passed the broken metal gates that had been pushed to the side at the entry to the country club. The brick walls that once held them were busted and covered in faded graffiti.

The next road narrowed, and he came to his destination, where he silenced the rumble of the engine.

Kasandra's dream house, once the envy of the Lakeview Country Club.

The estate once had a white three-story pillared front and a pitched roof, with a second-floor balcony that ran the full length of the mansion. It took years to build, and now it lay as a pile of wood and brick overrun by weeds and brush, nature reclaiming its land. It was much like the surrounding country club. Trees and shrubs had taken back the fairways and sand traps. There was nothing of its former glory. Not even memories of her grand parties could bring it back to life. Not anymore.

He sat at the steering wheel and sighed. So many memories. He glanced at the ruined home once more, then rested his forehead on the steering wheel. "I just need a minute before they all get here."

2

Twenty-Six Years Ago ...

TEDDY REREAD THE LETTER from the attorney's office, and then shook his head and crumpled it. A loud bang from down the hall caused Teddy to glance in that direction. Lane's office was just past one of Lane's favorite art pieces—a series of geometric shapes and lines arranged in random patterns done in orange and copper tones.

"Sorry, Daddy," Nicky yelped.

"Dammit, Nicholas," Lane shouted from his office.

"Lane! Enough," Teddy yelled back down the hall. "He's just a little boy. Leave him alone."

Nicky came scampering out of the office and down the hall in a beeline for Teddy. "Papabear," he cried and jumped into his arms. Teddy dropped the paper, trying to adjust for the full weight of Nicky. His son was almost too heavy to hold.

Teddy pulled the plastic Transformer's Halloween mask down over Nicky's face. "Don't you look great."

"Tank you. I'm Bumblebee," Nicky mumbled as he pushed the mask back up onto his head. He wiped his face with the back of his hand.

"Now what is my little Nickers getting into?"

Lane emerged from the office, blotting his white dress shirt with a towel. "Nicholas, get your butt over here." Lane pointed to the space in front of him with his free hand.

Nicky hugged Teddy tighter.

"What happen?" Teddy rested a hand on Nicky's back. Although he was becoming too old, he clearly needed to be held at the moment.

"He spilled coffee all over my shirt—"

"I just wanted to show Daddy my costume for tonight," Nick whimpered in Teddy's ear.

"And now I have a coffee stain, and I've got to meet clients in a half hour."

"Tonight? No way." Teddy shifted Nick in his arms. "You promised to go trick-or-treating with us."

Lane's eyes blazed. They looked so much like Nicky's, except Nick's were full of fear and Lane's full of rage. "Oh for—"

Teddy's eyes narrowed.

"One of us has to have a real job. And mine requires me to work tonight so you and Nicholas can go out and play."

"Wait a minute." Teddy put Nicky down, then shifted his own pirate shirt so that his stomach wasn't sticking out. "Sweetness, you go play in your room." Teddy smiled down at Nicholas and tousled his hair.

Nicky pulled the mask down and covered his ears as he ran off down the hall to his bedroom.

Do we really fight that much that Nicky would know to cover his ears?

Teddy's voice grew deeper as he marched over to Lane. "Now look. I have a real job. One that I'm appreciated for. It may not be in finance with a big corner office, but my client list is a hell of a lot better than yours." Teddy crossed his arms. "And remember, if it wasn't for my *real* job, you wouldn't have some of the clients you have."

"Screw this. You're a flipping hairdresser." Lane threw his hands in the air. "I'm done. I can't take this anymore. You coddle my son and—"

"Our son."

Lane stood taller and glared down at Teddy. "My son. My child. The one you constantly subvert my authority with. I'm done, Ted. This isn't working anymore. I want you out of my house. And take your fucking anxiety medicine with you. I don't want that shit around Nicholas. He's emotional enough thanks to you."

"Fuck you," Teddy snarled. "This is our—"

"My house. It's in my name, and I want you out. All we do is fight, and I'm sick of it. You can say goodbye to Nick in the morning, but I want you gone from here by tomorrow night. I'll hire a nanny and Nick will be just fine without you." Lane picked at the stain on his shirt with the towel still in his hand. "I'm calling my sister, and she can take Nicholas out tonight, so you can get your shit together." Lane turned to walk to the bedroom. "Now I'm going to be late for my meeting. Fuck."

Teddy stood frozen, his heart pounding in his chest as it shattered into a million pieces. This wasn't happening? Tears filled Teddy's eyes as he stared at the crumpled letter on the floor. He picked it up and read it again.

Mr. Granger,

We are sorry to inform you that your mother Mary Granger has passed away, and per her estate …

•　　　•　　　•

Not a cloud in the sky. The sun was warm on his face as he drove with the window open, even though the air was crisp. Slowing down at the Welcome to Lakeview sign, he checked out all the different club symbols. The Lions, 4-H, FFA, Kiwanis, Masons, and a few others he didn't recognize. He saw the town motto and stuck his tongue out at it. I'm already free. From his vantage point, the road wound down the hill toward town, where people rushed along the sidewalks, about their business. He nodded, ready to make his grand entrance.

Teddy checked his makeup and hair in the mirror, and then lowered the convertible top of his Mustang. *Please let my wig hold. Who cares if it was November and forty-something degrees out?* He wanted to make sure everyone saw him and knew that Theodore 'Teddilicious' Granger was back in town.

He headed down the main street, honking the car horn as he passed the few other vehicles on the road. He passed a tractor—*god, a tractor*—and winked at the farmer. The town was so cute with its diner, emporium, drugstore, and it even managed to still have a theater. People stopped and gawked as he waved and blew kisses.

"Yes, bitches, Teddilicious is home. I'm here to bring a rainbow to this dull boring-ass town."

He continued at a slow pace, making as large of a spectacle as possible. "Ah, small-town America, you gotta love it." He wasn't paying attention to what was behind him until he heard the siren and saw the flashing lights in his rearview mirror.

"Ah hell." He pulled over to the corner in front of CJ's Hardware and waited for the deputy to get out of his car.

"Fuck." Teddy pulled out his identification from the pink handbag on the passenger seat.

"Do you know why I pulled you over?"

Teddy peeked up at the officer—deputy, whatever. He was probably in his late twenties or early thirties, nice broad chest and a tight shirt and even tighter pants. His glasses were the typical reflective lenses, so Teddy couldn't see his eyes, but the stubble on his chin was easy enough to see. It's a solid look. The badge said G. Dempscy.

That name sounds familiar.

Deputy Dempscy puffed out his chest a bit.

"I asked, do you know why I pulled you over?"

Teddy tried not to roll his eyes.

Ugh, this good old boy thinks he's all that. Barf.

"Because I'm Teddilicious and you had to get a closer look?" Teddy flirted, batting his eyes for greater effect.

It might work.

Deputy Dempscy lowered his sunglasses to stare at Teddy. His brown eyes bore into Teddy and not in a good way. "License and registration, sir."

Teddy felt the venom in the deputy's words.

Ouch. Clearly, this man has no sense of humor.

Teddy handed him his license and the temporary registration for the vehicle.

"You were impeding traffic and disturbing the peace." Deputy Dempscy started writing a ticket.

Oh brother.

Several people were smiling and silently judging Teddy as they watched the deputy do his job. Teddy was sure they were getting a kick out of seeing the fag in drag get harassed by the cop. And Deputy Dempscy was putting on a show of exerting his authority—Teddy was sure—especially with how he was standing. *I wonder if there's a broom stuck up his ass.* It was like watching a peacock show off its plumage.

"Hey, Greg, why you picking on locals?" A woman with a stunningly bright smile and flowing brown hair called out as she exited the Main Street Emporium.

"Casey, don't go getting involved in police business and this ...person isn't a local," Deputy Dempscy said, tilting his head toward a woman with a blond little girl as they passed by. Teddy waved to the little girl who actually returned the gesture.

The breeze picked up and Teddy got a strong whiff of Polo that obviously emanated from Deputy Dempscy's. Teddy crinkled his nose at the smell but decided against saying anything.

Casey laughed. "Don't you recognize Ted Granger? You should. You ended up under him enough in football practice." She made her way over to the car, shifting her bag from one arm to another.

"Wait, Greg? Little Left Feet Greg?" Teddy finally recognized the name from school.

"Ah hell." Greg adjusted his hat with his free hand, his chest deflating along with his attitude.

Teddy's laugh filled the cool November air, and he hit the horn of his car by mistake. "Oh man, that was ages ago. You were such a scrawny little runt."

"I was a freshman, and I'm a lot bigger now." Greg frowned. "That was a long time ago."

Casey rested her yellow bag on the car. She leaned in and pointed at Teddy. "Love the hair and the car. Nice choice."

"Thanks." Teddy studied Casey a moment. "I don't think I—"

"I was just a kid back then. You played with my older brother Kevin. I would come watch him practice. Once I saw your eyes, I knew it was you." Casey smiled and flicked her hair over her shoulder. "Now I own and run the town's radio station, WLKV. Lakeview's home for music," she recited in a deeper voice, then coughed. She cleared her throat. "Man, you look different."

"Five-inch heels and a pink feather boa will do that."

Casey busted out laughing. "Not to mention that big black hair. Oh, honey, you wear it well."

"You know it, girly-girl. This big queen knows how to dress for travel and comfort." Teddy snapped his fingers.

"Excuse me. If you two don't mind." Greg held out a ticket.

"Don't be a dick, Greg," Casey said. "Look, if you tear that thing up, I'll put a good word in for you with Lisa. She's new enough to town not to know you're a special kind of stupid."

Greg stared down at the ticket, then over to Casey. Finally, he handed Teddy the ticket. "Do you want me to write you up as well, Casey?"

She rolled her eyes, "You don't have that kind of authority." She winked at Teddy. "Come on, Greg, a good word from me can go a long way."

"I don't need help with women. I do just fine," Greg said. "Especially with arms like these and a butt like mine." He strutted back to his patrol car.

Casey laughed and Teddy joined in.

"I'll talk to Tom about the ticket if you want. Deputy Dipshit thinks he's all that." Casey smiled and waved back at the cruiser as Greg got in. She looked back at Teddy. "Tom's the sheriff."

Teddy read the ticket. "Nah. I'll pay it. It's only my first day, and I'm sure there is going to be plenty of trouble I'll be getting into while I'm here." He narrowed his eyes a bit on her. "Okay, how did you know it was me? The eyes—seriously, not from where you were standing."

Casey's expression transformed into a frown that Teddy was sure didn't mean she had happiness and joy to spread. "I um … I-I'm sorry about your folks, especially your mom."

Teddy bit his bottom lip. "You knew my mom?"

Casey nodded. "I'd look in on her. We'd talk. She would show me pictures of you, even the ones of you in drag. When I saw the hair, the car, and the boa, I put it all together."

"Faggot," an old man grumbled loud enough to be heard by both Casey and Teddy. Teddy ignored it, but Casey glared at the man as he walked by, and his gaze quickly dropped to the sidewalk.

"Your mom was a good person ... well, to me."

Teddy felt his heart drop. *Of course she was nice to you.* "Thanks."

"Listen, why don't we have dinner tonight? We can catch up, and you can tell me what you've been up to." She pointed to Teddy's drag. "Clearly, you're going to be way more interesting than me, and this town can use a good dose of fun and culture. Nothing ever happens here. I swear the world outside this town might not even exist for some of these people." She flicked Teddy's boa. "You're the most excitement this place has probably ever seen."

Teddy felt his neck get warm. "Sounds like a plan. I'll get settled at the house, change, and meet you at seven tonight at the Lakeview Diner. It's still good, right?"

"Best place in town, but don't change. It's good to shake things up. Especially around here," Casey said as two older women walked by with scowls on their faces. "Afternoon, Ms. Maribel, Ms. Beatrice."

3

T HE JINGLE OF THE BELL on the door barely registered with Teddy. He had the TV going as he flipped through a People magazine. After a year, he still barely had any clients at his new shop. Casey, of course, and a few random folks, but mostly the good people of Lakeview treated Teddy's Trim like a den of vipers. The town thought they could wait Teddy out and eventually he would shutter his business and leave, but they were wrong. He had enough money, including that from his parent's investments, to keep this place running at a loss for as long as he wanted. As an additional "screw you" to the town, he bought the building his shop was in, under a false name, so the rent from the other stores helped cover the cost of his own and provided him with a good source of income.

If they only knew.

Despite the lack of customers, Teddy ensured his shop had everything. Including all the latest and greatest equipment. It wasn't quite a duplicate of his previous shop, but it still had his flavor and flare all around. The walls were covered in a warm gray color and the floor was a wood-patterned tile, giving a hardwood effect. It looked good and was a hell of a lot easier to clean. In the back, he had two shampoo stations and a sitting dryer. The sofa in the waiting area was large in a vibrant eggplant. The color and the couch provided an amazing contrast to the walls. Since there was no business, he only had two cutting stations, one on the left side and his station across on the right.

He heard someone clear their throat, and he glanced up from his magazine to discover a familiar older man with salt-and-pepper hair standing there.

"Oh hey." Teddy put down the reading material. "Sorry, I'm not used to anyone walking in."

"If this isn't a good time or you have appointments, I can come back," he said.

"Are you kidding, Doc?" Teddy laughed and stood. He pulled at the bottom of his shirt so it wasn't stuck in any of chunky bits.

"You know who I am?" Doc's eyebrows rose.

"Of course, I make it a point to know all the sexy older gents in town, and being the medical director at the hospital doesn't hurt either." Teddy held a finger to his temple. "Dr. Douglas Hudson married to Sally Hudson for twenty years, no children." He crossed arms over his chest. "The real question, Doc, is why are you here in my shop?"

Doc rubbed the back of his neck. "I need a haircut. Sally says I'm looking like a hippy, and I figured I would come here."

Teddy lifted a brow. "And this is the first time, in the year I've been open, that you needed a trim?" He tried to keep his voice level, but he was bitter about how the town treated him, not that he was making it easy for them. Still, people should be decent and respectful.

Including me.

Teddy took a breath, pushing the frustration away. It's not the doc's fault, and he's here now.

"I should have come sooner." Doc raked a hand through his hair. "Sally and I aren't happy with how folks have been treating you since you got here. She's gonna see how things go today and set up an appointment with you, if that's all right. Well, when she gets back from her business trip."

"Hmm, I see." Teddy pointed to the chair. "It's real nice of you to stop by, and I do appreciate it." Teddy's shoulders dropped and his face relaxed, allowing him to smile. "Well, come on then. Have a seat and let's get you all cleaned up for the wifey."

Doc sat in the chair as Teddy began his hair assessment. He tilted Doc's head left then right. Ran a comb through it. Examining him head-on so he could see what kind of style Doc's hair could handle. The man was handsome and had a distinguished forehead and symmetrical eyes. Of course the hints of a British accent didn't hurt either.

"I just need a trim." Doc pursed his lips.

Teddy tapped his finger to his mouth. "You don't know what you need, and I'm going to make you Teddilicious—"

"Teddy what?"

Teddy laughed. "Teddilicious, honey, trust me. You're gonna look amazing. You just hush and let me work." Teddy grinned, seeing the man's reflection in the mirror. "Your wife isn't going to be able to keep her hands off you when I'm finished."

Doc only nodded as Teddy draped him, then pulled him up out of the chair. He led him back for a shampoo. He had nothing better to do, so why not give this guy the full treatment? Especially if his wife would be judging the final product. Who knows, maybe he and his wife would become regulars, which would double the number of regulars Teddy currently had.

Working on people's hair always felt like home. It was like he had a purpose again. Especially since he hadn't heard from Lane or Nicky.

I hope Nicky is all right. I miss him.

•   •   •

"So, I'm going to have to hold a complete audit of the entire hospital to ensure we are HIPAA compliant. It's a pain the butt." Doc frowned at the mirror.

Over the two years since Doc walked into to his salon, Teddy had only noticed the slightest increase in gray. He offered to color it for him, but Doc always took a pass. Apparently, he felt like he'd earned it.

Teddy laughed at Doc. "This is why I stick to beauty. As long as I pay the government and keep my license up to date, I don't have to deal with that garbage." He tapped his lips as he looked at the doc sitting in his chair.

"You still have to keep training and your license has to be up to date. Not to mention keeping up with all the latest trends in hair," Doc said. "Last year, you were in New York, and the year prior, weren't you in LA?"

Teddy nodded as he spun Doc around to face him so he could trim his eyebrows. "Sure, but that was fun.

I mean HairWorld isn't like some stuffy medical conference. We get to party, Doc." He danced around the chair and bumped and ground a bit. "Get your freak on ... oh yes, baby."

Doc laughed. "Easy, Teddy. I don't want to have to treat you for a sprained ankle again."

"That wasn't my fault. Those heels weren't made for someone of my delicate physique."

"Whatever you say, Teddy." Doc chuckled.

Since the doc's first visit to the salon, Teddy, Doc, and Sally had become good friends. Doc would drop in every six weeks for a cut, and whenever Sally was around, she would make an appointment and get her hair cut, styled, and colored. It was a lucky break for Teddy, because once the doctor and Sally started talking Teddy up, a few more folks came to the salon. It took Teddy another year before he actually saw a profit for the shop. It was a small one, but it was there. The majority of the town still shunned him, but usually they kept to themselves and he did the same.

The door banged open. "Don't touch your hair, Jenny," a woman in dress slacks and a nice light-green blouse said as she pulled her daughter behind her. The girl was the sweetest little thing, but her face was red as she tried to hide behind her mother.

"Can you get gum out of her hair?" the woman demanded and tugged at Jenny's hand.

Teddy sighed as Doc smiled.

"Sure, but it'll have to wait until I'm finished with Dr. Hudson. About ten minutes?"

"Oh, Douglas, I'm sorry. It's just been a hell of a day and Jenny ..." She shook her head.

"I completely understand, Jacqueline," Doc said in a calm tone. He was using his perfect bedside-manner voice. Teddy had heard it when the doc had worked on his ankle. The man didn't judge anyone. He did his job and made people feel comfortable.

"Jenny, you sit here and don't cause any trouble." Jacqueline crossed back to the door. "I have to run to over to the Main Street Emporium to see if her Halloween costume is here."

"Mom, it's just gum." The young girl looked annoyed, sitting on the eggplant-colored sofa. "I'll be fine." Jenny wore a crisp school uniform, the skirt a green and white plaid with a white collared shirt topped by a green V-neck sweater. Other than the gum in her hair, Jenny looked no worse for wear.

Jacqueline glanced between Teddy and Doc. "If you need anything, you ask Dr. Hudson and you listen to him. You hear me?"

Jenny nodded and glanced at the floor.

"Douglas, I swear I'll be ten minutes. I promise."

"Don't ask me, Jackie. Ask Teddy. It's his shop."

Jacqueline glanced from Doc to Teddy. "I ... well ... you don't mind. I'm going to pay of course, whatever it costs. I just ... well, you're ... and Dr. Hudson is a ..."

"It's fine." Teddy waved his free hand. "I can have her all cleaned up for you." He forced what he hoped was a polite smile.

"Great." Jacqueline waved and rushed out the door.

All three watched the door close in complete silence. Finally, Teddy looked at Jenny. Her feet were bouncing off the couch. "So, that's your mom?"

Jenny nodded.

"Kind of all over the place."

Jenny nodded again.

"How'd you get the gum in your hair?"

"Stupid Joey Collins. He thought it was funny."

"What a jerk," Teddy said.

"Yep, he's mean." Jenny kicked her feet against the couch as she watched Teddy and Doc. "I called him a fart face and pushed him in the mud."

Doc's lips quivered as he tried to cover his laugh, but Teddy couldn't help it and chuckled. Jenny followed suit. Teddy went back to Doc's hair and finished him up as quickly as possible so that he could work on Jenny's. The gum wasn't going to be the problem. It was making sure that she had a cute haircut once he cut it out.

By the time Jacqueline got back, Jenny was sitting in Teddy's chair happily chatting away about how she was going to be the Little Mermaid for Halloween and how it would be super cool if Teddy could dye her hair red. For the briefest of moments, Teddy considered it until he saw Doc shake his head no.

Sometimes the doc is just no fun.

"I really appreciate what a nice job you did." Jacqueline reached for her wallet inside her purse.

"Mommy, can Mr. Teddy do my hair all the time?" Jenny asked. She shook her head and grinned in the mirror as her hair flopped back and forth.

"I don't know." Jacqueline handed Teddy the cash for the cut. "He seems awfully busy."

Teddy beamed down at the little girl and winked. "Nonsense, sweetness, you can get your hair done anytime you want." He crossed over to the counter with his appointment book and put the money in the drawer. "In fact, why don't you come back before you go trick-or-treating and I'll make you look just like the Little Mermaid?"

"Oh you don't have to—"

"It's my treat, and tell you what, Jackie. When she comes, I'll even give your hair a blowout and style at no charge."

"He does amazing work, Jackie. Sally only lets Teddy touch her hair now. He's a magician, and once everyone sees his work at the country club, you'll be the talk of the town."

"Well, I—"

"Excellent." Teddy wrapped an arm around Jackie's waist as he escorted her and Jenny to the door. "See you in a few days." He waved and closed the door behind them.

"Think she'll show up?" Teddy peeked over his shoulder at Doc.

"Oh, I'll make sure of it. Plus, Jenny can be a spitfire when she wants to be."

"That shy sweet little girl? Poor woman doesn't stand a chance, does she?"

They both laughed.

•　　•　　•

Teddy flipped the closed sign on his shop door and headed back to his small office. He still had to place a supply order and figure out the new accounting software he'd ordered. Gradually, more and more people were coming around to his salon and his days seemed to be getting busier. It was nice. Having some of the country club crowd now as clients went a long way to help his reputation in town.

He cracked his neck and took a deep breath. There was a sudden tap on the glass door and Teddy jumped.

"So much for a quiet evening," he mumbled and turned to see a tall woman with broader than normal shoulders standing there. Every other part of her screamed runway model or fashion diva, but even for the Hamptons, the hat and big glasses were a bit much. She looked out of place as Bud's tractor-trailer drove past her.

"I'm closed." He pointed to the sign on the door.

"Oh please." She waved her hands.

"Fine." He walked over to the door and unlocked it, and she stormed in.

"Oh thank Christ. I don't know what to do. It's awful, just awful." She fanned her face and walked to the couch where she collapsed onto it. "Do you—oh please, may I have a cup of water?"

"Um ... sure." Teddy walked over to the coffee station and poured the woman a glass of water. It was warm, but it would have to do. "Here ya go."

She took the water and drank it greedily. "I just ... It's awful." She took another sip. "You know this is warm, right? You don't happen to have any ice, do you?" She held out the glass and then took it back. "I'm sorry that was rude, but ice would be lovely."

Teddy held up his hand. "Sorry, no ice. Now, what's awful?"

The woman shrugged, then glanced around the salon, running a hand nervously over the sofa she was sitting on. "Oh I can't ... can I ... oh but I have to." She pulled off her glasses and looked him dead in the eyes. "I can't have you laughing at me, I need help. I'm in serious trouble."

Teddy's heart skipped a beat, and for a moment, he wondered if he should call the sheriff or Lisa or even Greg for this woman. "Are you sure you need my help?"

"You're the only one. I can't trust that hack of a barber the street over. God in heaven, it's just awful."

"I'll do what I can."

She nodded. With tears in her eyes, she started, "I waited until it was dark and you were about to close. I just couldn't risk anyone seeing me like this." She pulled off the hat and almost burst into tears.

Teddy looked at the hair beneath. Other than a case of hat hair and maybe the color being a bit too harsh for her skin tone, he didn't see anything wrong. "What is it?"

"Oh my God!" she squealed. "It's awful. Look at this cut. I'm having my first dinner at the country club and look at my hair. It's awful. It makes my cheeks look fat and it shows my neck. I hate people seeing my neck. It's not my best feature." She fanned herself. "Oh, please, may I have another glass of water? You sure you don't have any ice?"

Teddy tried hard not to roll his eyes. This woman was way over the top, even for him. Which made her a thousand times over the top for this town. Where had she come from? How had he never run into her before? And why did it have to be tonight?

"They just finished the construction on my new home. Two years. It took two years." She held up two fingers. "Well, I had to wait for the fixtures from Italy, but still two years. Oh God." She continued to wave her hand to fan herself. "I'm supposed to have this party tomorrow, but the butcher in Kansas City did this to me." She adjusted how she was sitting on the sofa and fussed with her skirt. "I've been staying there while they've been working on my little place. It's a small place right off hole nine. Oh I can't wait for everyone to see it. But, I can't let people see me like this. It's awful. Just awful." She finished the new glass of water Teddy had brought her. "I'm Kasandra St. Martin, by the way. Can you fix it? Can you make me look human again? I'll pay—"

"Okay, hold up, Miss Thing. I need you to take a breath and relax." Teddy took her hat, scarf—where the hell did the scarf come from—and glasses she handed him. "Let's get you shampooed, and I'll see what I can do. But you have to understand emergency work after-hours like this doesn't come cheap."

"Well, I should hope not." She handed him her purse. "I know this is small-town America, but I expect the best and clearly I can pay for it." She examined the diamond ring on her hand.

And pay for it you shall.

4

"**O**H MY GOSH, GREG, you're awful." Lisa sipped her iced tea while shaking her head.

Teddy loved coming to the diner and hanging out with Casey, Lisa, and Greg. It took quite a few years, but finally Greg had come around, and Teddy discovered he actually liked the guy. They could talk football, which was kind of nice, especially since Teddy knew way more than Greg. It amazed him that it had been five years since he moved back to town.

"If I'm so awful, then why does everyone cheer and get up and dance?" He took a bite of a chicken wing, getting some sauce on his stubble-covered chin, and grabbed his napkin to wipe it off.

"It's because you're so awful." Casey flipped her hair over her shoulder. "It's the only way to keep from having to hear your singing."

"Or watching your dancing," Lisa added as she adjusted her deputy's shirt over her heavy bosom. "Especially after you drink."

Teddy laughed and reached for a chicken wing.

"Come on, man, you might be a homo, but can't you help me out here? We're bros." Greg went for another wing.

Lisa slugged Greg in the arm as Casey pulled the basket of wings away from him.

"Homo? Really?" Teddy dropped the wing on his plate. "Listen, Deputy Dipshit, I'll come to your aid when you earn it."

"Sorry," Greg said as he tried to pull the basket back over, but Casey wouldn't let go. He called over his shoulder, "Hey, Dee, can you be a love and get me a basket of wings and maybe some of your onion rings?"

"What did you do?" Dee called back. "You better not be letting your mouth place bets that your butt can't cash."

Teddy pointed and mock-laughed at Greg.

"Nothing. They're being mean to me," Greg whined.

"Of course they are, boo-boo. Hey, Bill, can do me up wings and rings for the deputy? He ain't playing nice again."

Casey, Lisa, and Teddy all burst out laughing.

"Man, you guys suck," Greg said, then shut his eyes and waved his hands in front of him. "Wait! Please, Teddy, don't say it."

Teddy waggled his eyebrows and blew Greg a kiss.

"Anyway, so did we want to check out the new movie at the theater tonight?" Casey kept a hand on the basket so that Greg couldn't get to them.

"Deputy Anderson, come back," Lisa's radio squawked. Everyone at the table froze.

Lisa sighed and picked up her shoulder mic. "This is Deputy Anderson. Over."

"Lisa, it's Tom. I need you to go over to Dr. Phuong's greenhouse. She's saying that some kids have broken in and messed with her plants again. Over."

"10-4, I'll be there in fifteen. Over and out." Lisa finished off her iced tea. "Well, so much for my quiet night."

"Oh man, I'm so glad Tom called you." Greg shook his head. "That Dr. Phuong is freaky. I think she likes her plants way more than people."

"Well, if it was a choice between you and her plants, I would pick her plants too." Casey took her hand off the basket of wings and Greg snatched them back. "Hey!"

Greg laughed. He took a wing and bit into it.

"Erica's not too bad." Teddy sipped his diet pop. "She's a little odd, but who isn't? I love cutting her hair. It's amazing. So soft. She says it's some plant extract, but darn if I know what it is. Plus, it's hard when you're new to town. People make all kinds of judgments." He glared at Greg.

"Oh, man, let it go. That ticket was like forever ago." Greg sighed.

"Anyway, children, I think she has a thing for the sheriff." Lisa stood and adjusted her utility belt. "She's the only person I know in town who has someone breaking into her building at least once a week. I mean come on. Shit like that doesn't happen here in this town."

"Well, if she has a thing for the sheriff, then why are you going and not him?" Casey pushed Teddy over so she could get a little more room now that Lisa was leaving. "Plus, I think she has a thing for Dr. Hudson."

Dee placed the fresh basket of wings on the table along with an order of onion rings. "Tom and Erica had lunch here the other day. And you all know better than to gossip. It's rude." Dee walked off with a laugh.

"No way." Greg turned his head to see if she was going to say any more.

"Shut up," Casey remarked.

"I knew it." Lisa peeked down at her watch. "Ugh. I need to go take care of this. Or the sheriff is gonna bust my butt, especially if Erica calls back and no one has come over yet." She grabbed a fresh onion ring and stuffed it in her mouth. "But I leave it up to the three of you to pump Dee for information, and I want a full report when I get back."

"Assuming we're going to be here," Teddy said. "I really want to see the new Disney movie." He nabbed a couple of rings and put them on his small plate.

"Ugh, Of course you do." Greg shook his head.

"How about we meet up for drinks at Jax's after the movie?" Casey offered, dipping a wing in some blue cheese dressing.

"If I have to sit through a Disney flick, I'm gonna need a beer or ten." Greg leaned back in his chair and stretched out his arms.

"Oh poor baby." Teddy reached out and tweaked Greg's nipple through his shirt.

Greg swatted Teddy's hand. "Knock it off."

"So, perky." Teddy giggled and poked at Greg, then laughed even harder.

"Okay, I'm out of here. Jax's after the movie. I'll be waiting. Oh and, Teddy, he only wants you to stop 'cause it gives him a stiffy," Lisa teased and her green-eyed gaze dropped to Greg's crotch before she headed for the door with a wave over her shoulder.

"And how would you know?" Greg called, and then frowned. "Wait. I'm not saying that happens when he does that. I just—"

Teddy and Casey laughed.

•   •   •

The sun shone through the large plate-glass window as Teddy took another bite of his salad. As he started to chew, he made a face.

I want a milkshake and burger, but I'm having rabbit food. Ugh.

Teddy glanced around the diner. The lunch rush was over, and he could enjoy his meal in peace. That was the benefit of arranging his own schedule. He took another nibble of his salad as the bell above the door jingled.

Kasandra strutted in and glanced around. Her gaze narrowed on Teddy a second before she made a beeline straight for him.

"Oh thank Christ." She slid into the chair in front of him, pulled off her scarf, and removed her oversized glasses.

"Hey there, Miss Thing." Teddy put down his fork, knowing that he wouldn't be able to eat until Kasandra said whatever she wanted to tell him or ordered her own meal, and even then, he wasn't sure there would be a chance to finish.

She had a frown on her face. "Teddy, can we talk?" Her voice was different today, more serious and less fluttery like a butterfly.

Dee walked over. "What can I getcha?" She held out a menu to Kasandra and put down a glass of water with a ton of ice.

"I'll just have what Teddy's having—a salad, please," Kasandra said, not taking the menu.

Dee nodded and headed back to the kitchen.

"We're friends right?" Kasandra asked, her gaze focused on Teddy's.

"Sure. What's up?" He leaned forward to give her all his attention.

Everyone in the diner seemed to vanish until it was just the two of them. Kasandra didn't have serious conversations. Everything about her was superficial. Her small house on the country club was the largest home the homeowner's association would allow. Her clothes were the latest fashion, her car—in the year since she officially moved to town—had been turned in and exchanged for the newest model twice. Even her parties were the best, with only the right people. He managed to get an invite because he understood her hair and he could make Kasandra look amazing, for which she was grateful.

"Seriously, Teddy, are we friends? I don't have any here. Sure, there are people I'm social with, but not friends."

He thought a moment about their conversations when they were alone in the shop and he was doing her hair. Were they friends? He wasn't so sure, but Kasandra needed a friend and he was going to be hers.

"Yes, Kas, we're friends," Teddy finally said and took a sip of water.

"As my friend, I need your help." Kasandra pulled out a piece of paper. The seals showed it was some kind of legal document. She handed it over to him.

Teddy took the letter, opened it, and began to read.

Kasandra sat there, clicking her nails and glancing around the diner. During the time it took Teddy to read the letter, Dee arrived, put down the salad, and walked over to a group of men who had just finished their shift at CAGE.

Teddy folded up the letter and handed it back to Kasandra. She slipped it back into her purse, watching him. His face grew cool and he felt his heart beating faster. He reached for his own glass of water and sipped it.

"Well?" she asked.

Teddy nodded. "I don't know. Why didn't you take care of this in California?"

"I thought I had. All the documents were changed, but now they are hung up with the birth certificate. And I don't know what to do. I swear I thought it was all sorted out." Tears pooled in her eyes, and she quickly grabbed the napkin and dabbed them.

Teddy reached out and took her hand. "We'll take care of this. I know a lawyer in Kansas City. I'm pretty sure he can help."

"Teddy, if anyone finds out here in town, they'll lynch me. I moved here because I knew that I needed the break and I had the money to live the life I wanted. To live my life as the real me. The life I could have never had out there."

"Then why all the pretense? Miss Thing, you are way over-the-top, even for me, and this town doesn't look fondly on different. Why draw any more attention to yourself?"

The tears had finally stopped, and she took a deep breath. "I knew it would be difficult anywhere, but I figured if I came here and acted this way, people wouldn't notice the other smaller things."

"Like the broad shoulders and scars on the neck?" Teddy asked.

She nodded.

"Well, honestly, you look amazing. So, maybe, you know, just be yourself a little more. You don't have to be some caricature for anyone. It'll be better for you to just be who you are instead of some over-the-top diva."

She started to speak, and Teddy patted her hand. "Be like this more often. Be real with people. You're beautiful, and no one will ever be able to tell that you"—he lowered his voice even more—"transitioned. Now, what about your meds and checkups and stuff like that? You got a doctor in Kansas City?"

"No. Dr. Hudson knows. He does my checkups and keeps everything very confidential. It saves me from having to go to KC. That man is a dream."

Teddy chuckled.

Well, he can certainly keep a secret.

"Look, I'll call my friend and set up an appointment for next week. We can make a day of it and go shopping and hang out. It'll be fun."

"You'll do that for me? And you'll keep my secret?" Kasandra took a shaky breath, reached for her water, and sipped it.

"Your secret isn't mine to tell. Plus, Lakeview has a way of holding onto secrets and never letting them go." Teddy made a face down at their salads. He glanced over his shoulder to the counter. "Hey, Dee, can we get some chicken tenders and fries. These salads need a pick-me-up."

"You got it, Teddy."

"And two chocolate shakes," Kasandra called. "Teddy and I are having a real lunch."

Teddy laughed. "Oh, I love your style, Miss Thing."

•   •   •

Teddy picked at his salad. The diner really did have the best food, but considering all he tried to eat was salad these days, it didn't matter. Ugh! Trying to lose weight sucks. This year's goal was to lose twenty pounds.

"Men." Casey shook her head. "Why do we even bother?"

"Because some of them are sexy as hell," Kasandra said.

"And it's better than sleeping alone," Teddy said.

"And I think I need to head back to the hospital." Doc made to grab for his hat and jacket.

Teddy pointed to where the doctor sat. "Don't even try it, Doc. I told Sally I would make sure you ate and took some time away from work."

"What? I ate and I took a break," Doc said.

"You started your day at six thirty this morning and it's now almost seven forty in the evening, and I know for a fact you didn't take lunch." Teddy continued to point at the seat and the doctor.

"How do you—"

"Never underestimate the power of the Teddy." Teddy waved his hands in front of him. "I know and see all."

"Fine." Doc leaned back in the chair. "You know it's been proven we have a biological need to make connections with other people. The more connected we become, the harder it is to lose those relationships."

Kasandra's brows furrowed. "Oh trust me, I can cut ties like no body's business. Once you cross me, you are dead to me." She snapped her fingers to emphasize her point.

"Maybe, so, but I bet it's not easy." Doc sipped his coffee.

"Well, I think I'm going to have to dump Sam. He's just ...ugh ... annoying." Casey frowned. "Why can't I meet a guy like you, Teddy?"

"For one, I'm gay and that would do you no good. For two, could you imagine the world with two Teddies? I don't think we could survive."

"I agree. I think one of you is enough." Doc picked at the remains of his mashed potatoes and meatloaf.

"Hey, that's not nice." Teddy puffed out his bottom lip.

Doc shook his head. "You know what I mean."

The door jingled, and Tom walked in and took off his hat, revealing a bald head. He scanned the room and crossed over to the counter. If the scanning of the room didn't give it away, then his stance did. He was 100 percent former Marine.

"You have my order ready, Dee?" He rested his hat on the counter and reached down to adjust his utility belt, then rested his hand on his gun.

"Hey, Sheriff, come join us." Teddy waved. It was amazing that his utility belt fit him at all with as thin as he was, plus he had no butt whatsoever to help hold it up. Still, he wasn't an awful-looking man, just tall and thin.

And we all know what that means.

He smirked at the evil thought and quickly glanced to the front of the sheriff's pants.

"Should I be worried that I see the four of you together?" Tom pointed at them. His face barely changed expressions from its typical stoic nature.

"Who us? Cause trouble? Never." Kasandra beamed with a flourish of her hand.

"Indeed," Tom said.

"Here's your order, Sheriff." Dee passed everything over in various bags.

"Thanks, Dee." Tom took the parcels.

Dee headed over to check on her other customers.

"I'm gonna have to pass on the offer to join you," Tom said. "We have work down at the station."

"Well, poo." Teddy frowned.

"Everything okay, Sheriff?" Casey asked. "Do we need to get a message out or something?"

"No, everything's fine, but I would like to check in about the emergency procedures you have. Anything can happen, and it's always good to be prepared."

"Sure thing, Sheriff," Casey said.

"Have a good night." Tom put on his hat and headed out the diner door.

"You know even when he comes to the salon for a head shave, he hardly says anything." Teddy sipped his diet pop.

"Some people are just private." Kasandra eyed Teddy.

"True, but I don't know." Teddy played with his straw. "It just seems like it's something else. It's kind of the same thing with Erica."

"Teddy, not everyone can be like you," Doc said. "Is that all you three do is gossip about people here in town?"

"Yep, and you should hear what we say about you, Doc." Casey laughed.

The bell on the diner door jingled again as it opened. A teenager in a hoodie walked in. The breeze from the door caused a chill to run down Teddy's back as he turned to Casey, Kasandra, and Doc.

"You know, what about having a Halloween Party this year?"

"Oh I love parties." Kasandra clapped. "We can have it at my house."

"Of course we can." Casey laughed. "Any excuse for a party."

"Excuse me," the kid in the hoodie said. He couldn't be more than fifteen.

"What's up, cutie? You get lost?" Teddy scanned the young man up and down.

"Are you Ted—Teddy Granger?" the kid said.

Doc, Kasandra, and Casey all glanced at Teddy.

Teddy's eyes narrowed. "I am."

The boy pulled off his hoodie. He had a black eye and a dimpled chin, his hair was long and wavy and in desperate need of a cut. But that didn't matter to Teddy. The chair he had been sitting on was shoved back and hit the wall as he rushed over and grabbed the boy, hugging him with all his heart.

"Oh God. Nicky."

"Pappabear." The boy wrapped his arms around Teddy and hugged him back. "Why did you leave me with him? Why didn't you take me? You left me trapped." Nicky's words muffled against Teddy's shoulder.

5

"**I** DON'T SEE WHAT THE BIG DEAL IS. It was one beer," Nick said as he continued to sweep Teddy's salon.

Nick had only been there for six months, and Teddy already had him cleaning the shop as part of his grounding. He also had him cleaning and waxing his pink Mustang in front of the shop while "It's Raining Men" played. Ever since he moved, Nick had stumbled into the wrong clique at school. Doc said it was an adjustment for both of them and offered to call in a colleague of his who specialized in child psychology to work with them during this time of transition. He also said that the cleaning of the car might not have been the best form of punishment.

Maybe I should take the doc up on his offer for the psychologist.

"The big deal is, you're a minor." Teddy huffed, both hands on his hips. "You're lucky it was Greg who found you out there. What have I told you about messing around Dr. Phuong's greenhouse? Erica is very particular about her experiments."

"But nothing happened." Nick stopped and leaned on the broom.

"That's not the point. You were drinking and got caught."

"So, if we didn't get caught, that would be okay?" Nick said with a raised eyebrow.

"Don't be cute. Do you have any idea what I had to do to get your dad to agree to let you move here? Of course, it helped that he gave you that shiner. The louse. You're lucky I've got such a good lawyer. Well, better than your dad's and that Tom offered to file an official report."

"I know. You're a wonderful father, and I appreciate all that you've done, blah-blah-blah."

"Hey! Watch it." Teddy pointed. "I can't say I like this attitude of yours, and I'm really no fan of your buddies."

"Come on, Teddy ..."

Teddy crossed his arms over his chest and raised his eyebrows.

What the hell happened to the sweet kid he left all those years ago? Was Lane really that bad of a father? Of course he was.

Teddy shook his head.

"I'm not gonna call you Papabear. I'm not a kid anymore. It makes me feel silly."

"Well, you're not gonna call me Teddy. I expect better from you and I deserve better."

"How about Pops? I know—Oldman?" Nick laughed. "I've seen your drag wigs—how about Big Momma?"

"I'll Oldman you." Teddy made a run for the broom. "Give me that broom."

"You're mad about Oldman and not Big Momma." Nick laughed.

Teddy took off after Nick, but Nick was quicker. He held tight to the broom and ran for the front door just as it opened and Jenny walked in with a bag of chips and a pop. The collision was fast and the proceeding thud echoed through the shop.

"Fuck," Nick said as he landed on his butt. He pushed the broom away so it didn't hit him or the little girl.

"Language, Nick!" Teddy rushed to Jenny on the floor. "Oh, Jenny. Honey, you okay?" He helped her up.

"I'm fine." She looked at her chips and pop on the ground. The pop was spilling on Teddy's tile floor and the chips were sprawled all the way to the couch.

Nick stood up and dusted off his pants. "You okay?"

She nodded and smiled at him. Her doe eyes watching him.

"Go get the mop," Teddy demanded and pointed as he took Jenny over to the couch.

"Yes, sir." Nick headed to the back of the shop and the janitor's closet.

Jenny watched him walk off but didn't say anything. It was kind of sweet.

"With as grounded as that boy is, he's not going to be leaving the house till he's well into his thirties." Teddy shook his head. They would address the drinking and other issues later that night when they got home.

"Oh, don't get him in trouble. It was my fault. I should have been paying attention to where I was going." Jenny fumbled with her school uniform, her gaze falling to the floor as she melted deeper into the couch.

"Oh Nick's not in trouble for that." Teddy chuckled. "Although it hasn't helped his case."

"Okay."

Teddy stood up and picked up the broom and glanced to the back of the shop. What was so difficult about finding the mop and grabbing the bucket? He went to his counter and pulled out a towel.

I swear that boy is a pain in the ass.

"I haven't seen you in a while, sweetness. Everything okay at home?" Teddy smiled and then glanced at the pop as it slowly meandered along the floor. He picked up the can and tossed the towel on the floor to cover the spill.

"It's fine, Mr. Teddy." Jenny flattened her skirt. "I've just been busy at school and dance lessons, but I'll come by more. Not like my folks miss me."

"Oh now don't say that. They're just busy." He held the can.

"I suppose."

"What brings you by today?"

"Mr. Teddy, I wanted to know if I could borrow some of your glitter spray for my school project," Jenny asked, still picking at her skirt.

"Of course, sweetness. What's your project?"

"We all have to do a report on the coming meteor shower, and I thought your glitter spray would make a fun background for my drawing. My mom didn't have time to get it, so I figured I would ask you, 'cause you know everything."

"Teddy. I can't find the bucket," Nick yelled from the back of the salon.

"Good lord." Teddy started across the shop, still holding the can. "You wait right there, Jenny. I'll get the spray for you and another pop. Or maybe I'll have Nick take you down to the diner for a milkshake."

"What?" Nick called.

Oh, that he hears.

"Oh that would be wonderful." Jenny's voice got soft and dreamy like all girls when they had a crush.

And some boys.

•   •   •

The only topic of conversation in town was the upcoming meteor shower. It was all anyone talked about at Teddy's salon, and now it was the only thing people were talking about at the diner. Well, that and Kasandra's Meteor Shower Viewing party. If you asked Teddy, it was a lot of fuss for a bunch of lights in the sky, but who was he to begrudge people of their fun? Plus, another party at Kasandra's would be a blast.

Teddy fiddled with his drink as he peered around the diner. It seemed busier than normal, but then again, it was almost the dinner rush, so more folks were coming in for their supper. It was odd for him to be there at a peak time. Teddy did his best to avoid the rush. The crowds didn't help his anxiety and, it made it better to chat and enjoy his meal, especially when it was just him and Nicky.

"I've got the caterers all set, the band of course, and I've rented, from Kansas City, several telescopes so everyone should be able to scope out the sky if they want." Kasandra reviewed her list, her black-framed glasses resting on the tip of her nose.

"Sounds good." Teddy played with the straw of his diet pop.

"Do you think I should have a Mashed Potato Bar or a Risotto Bar?" Kasandra tapped the pencil to her chin. "I kind of want to have a grilled Reuben station too, but I'm worried if that will be too much. What do you think? I mean, I know food and booze make the party, but I want everyone to see the show that Mother Nature is providing."

Teddy continued glancing out the window at the busy street.

"I know." Kasandra pointed to her pad. "I'm going to have all the serving staff covered in body paint, and then we can lick the food right off them."

"What?" Teddy's head snapped back at her.

Kasandra put down her notepad. "Okay, what's going on? You haven't listened to a single thing I've been saying. Are you still worried about Nick?"

Teddy met her gaze. "He went from the sweet little boy to this stubborn, pigheaded, troublemaker of a teen. I don't know what to do. Most of the time, he's off with those loser friends of his, and I know they are causing trouble at Erica's lab and greenhouse. But he won't talk to me." He took a sip of his drink. "You know Greg has caught them out there at least four times this last month, even after I grounded him. He's been sneaking out."

Kasandra laughed as she reached out for Teddy's arm. "Being a parent isn't easy. You should know that. You raised that boy for all those years."

A smirk crossed Teddy's lips as he shook his head, "But back then, if he got out of line, I could sic Lane on him. Now, it's only me. I don't like being the bad guy."

"Maybe you need to try some tough love," Kasandra said. "Have the sheriff lock him and his friends up overnight. Teach him a lesson and let him know there are consequences for his actions." She reached for her iced tea and sipped it.

"I don't know about that. He's been through a lot and he's just a baby."

"Look, Teddy, Lord knows I had issues with my family and they had issues with me, but I never walked all over them like Nick is doing to you. He's taking advantage of that great big heart of yours."

Teddy's gaze dropped to the table with his half-eaten club sandwich. "I can talk to Greg and Lisa and see if maybe they can scare them." His heart dropped at the idea, but something needed to change. He and Nick had to find a middle ground.

"I'm sure it'll be fine." Kasandra patted Teddy's hand, then gave it a quick squeeze. "He's just got some adjusting to do. Look, I'm having the party for everyone including the rugrats and anklebiters, not to mention the teens, so at least you'll know where he is." Kasandra picked up her notepad and pencil. "God, that reminds me, I've got to remember to have the furniture scotchguarded and I'll need to set up the cleaners for the next day."

She slammed the pad down on the table. "Oh my God. I've got it."

"What?" Teddy asked, looking around.

"A masquerade. It should totally be a masquerade ball. It'll be a little early for Halloween but only by a few weeks." She clapped her hands. "What do you think? It would be so much fun."

Teddy shook his head. "Good luck with that."

"You don't think—"

"There you are." Casey plopped down in the booth next to Teddy and grabbed some of his uneaten fries.

Teddy hadn't even heard her walk up. It was like she was a ghost. "Hey, girly-girl, what's up?" He forced what he was hoping was a happy face. If he was honest, he was feeling better after chatting with Kasandra. Maybe a good scare was what Nick needed, and Lisa and Greg would be perfect for it. "I thought you were going to be at the radio station today?"

"I was, but I got Jason, my intern, there right now." Casey took a few more fries and leaned back in the chair. "I love having interns. I can get them to do all the work, and I don't have to pay them shit. It's the best." Casey laughed.

"You're just wrong."

"What? I give them room and board, plus they get work experience. It's not that bad. Jason even gets his own evening show, which a lot of places won't do, but I offer." She shrugged. "How else do you expect me to have a life? I can't do it myself, and Misty is only part-time."

"I thought you were working on getting more advertising to hire more staff?" Teddy picked up his sandwich and took a bite.

"I am. I'm hoping with that money I can upgrade the station's electronics and tower. If I do that, I'll have a farther range, which will hopefully get me more advertising." She sighed. "Right now, I'm lucky to have all of Lakeview in my listening audience with as outdated as my equipment is."

"You'll get there," Kasandra said.

"If it helps, I can up my advertising," Teddy said. "Not a lot, but I can buy more time."

"Ah thanks, Teddybear." Casey gave him a side hug.

"Wait! You're going to be at the party, right?" Kasandra leaned in. "You have to be. I'll die if you're not there."

"Of course I'll be there, relax." Casey took a sip of Teddy's drink. "Misty and Jason will be running things for the night." She massaged her hands. "Although I'm wondering if I should be at the station in case something happens."

"Honey—" Kasandra pointed the pencil at her. "—it's a bunch of space dust that is going to brighten the skies here in the Midwest. What could possibly go wrong?"

•　　•　　•

"Come on, Pops. Let me drive the car once. Just around the block?" Nick said from the passenger seat of Teddy's pink Mustang as they pulled up to Kasandra's house. "Wow. This is her house?"

Teddy nodded and stopped at the valet. *Of course Kasandra has valets for the night.* "I thought you'd been … oh, right, you were too cool to come to her Labor Day party."

"Well, if I knew it looked like this, I would have. I bet she's got a pool back there?"

"Of course and it's lovely." The engine rumbled as he put it in park and turned it off, leaving the keys in the ignition for the valet. "Come on."

"One spin?" Nick asked with big eyes and a puffed-out bottom lip.

"You're still on probation. Now move." Teddy got out of the car and faced the sky as it danced with blue and purple lights. "Amazing. Have you ever seen anything like it?"

"Nope." Nick gazed up. "Mr. Hernandez in science class says it's the solar radiation bouncing off our magnetic field, or something like that. The whole Midwest is supposed to see these lights."

"You learned that in school?"

"Hey. I pay attention."

Teddy chuckled as they made their way up to the solid walnut doors. The graceful metal work in the windows and the patterned wood inlays were unlike anything Teddy had seen. Every time he walked through the doors, he felt like he was entering a dream.

Nick adjusted his jacket and tie.

Teddy stopped him and readjusted the black tie and dusted off the shoulders. Kasandra might not have gotten her masquerade ball, but she insisted that the event be formal, which meant jackets and ties for the men and cocktail dresses for the women.

Nick fussed under Teddy's hands. "You should have worn your royal blue cocktail dress. You always got a lot of compliments on that."

"I thought about it, but I didn't want to make things uncomfortable for folks. Plus, I like Kasandra and I didn't want to upstage her with my beauty." Teddy tilted his head staring at Nick. "If I didn't know any better, I would say you were almost respectable."

"Gee thanks." Nick pulled at Teddy's tie.

After Teddy adjusted his tie and jacket, they made their way into the grand foyer. Flowers and people were everywhere. He was glad he took his medicine tonight, especially with all the people. The house had the smell of lilies and roses and everything from the marble floors to the dual staircases shone. Light jazz filled the home through hidden speakers. The view went all the way through the house to the glass wall of doors that were open to the viewing area where everyone would be later to see the meteor shower.

"This is really cool," Nick said as a server walked by with a tray of champagne. He nabbed one, which Teddy quickly took from his hand.

"Thank you." Teddy's voice was sharp. He took a sip.

Nick pursed his lips.

"Please, Nick, just for tonight, don't get into any trouble. I really want to have a lovely evening with my handsome son and friends." Teddy took another sip of the champagne.

"There are my handsome men." Kasandra's voice cut through all the rest of the noise in the house.

Teddy turned and waved. She wore a black cocktail dress with blue sapphire jewelry, and her hair, which was done up in a French braid, highlighted all her best features. She was stunning, and her heels made Teddy jealous.

"You look beautiful." He hugged her.

"You're really pretty, Ms. St. Martin." Nick's eyes never made it past her ample cleavage.

She paid big bucks for those boobs. People better enjoy them.

"Ah, aren't you sweet." Kasandra pinched Nick's cheek and pulled his face up. "I have the pool house all set up for the young adults, so why don't you head out there and leave all us adults to our boring talk? We'll see you for the meteor shower."

Nick, not needing any more encouragement, made his way through the crowd and was gone.

"He really is a good boy." Kasandra took Teddy's hand. "Now don't worry about the booze. The staff knows not to give them anything and all the adult beverages are locked up and kept safe so there will be no sneaking any."

"You sure about that, Miss Thing?"

"Oh, please," Kasandra patted his arm. "I remember what I had to do to get my hands on liquor when I was their age, and so I made it teenage-me proof." She chuckled.

Teddy nodded and had another sip of his drink. "Thank you."

"Of course. Now let's get our party on." Kasandra moved them deeper into the house.

After Kasandra and Teddy flitted about together through Kasandra's home, she left Teddy on his own. She is the hostess after all. He made his way around the various groups, finding Doc chatting with the sheriff and Erica.

"Teddy." Doc reached out to shake hands. "Good to see you."

"And you, Doc." Teddy took the offered hand. "You letting Lisa and Greg protect the town tonight, Sheriff?"

Tom nodded. He was in a gray suit with black tie. No hat and no utility belt. "I thought I could use the break and Erica needed to get her mind off her plants."

"That's not fair." Erica pouted, looking stunning in an emerald dress that hugged her curves nicely. "I'm just worried what affect the meteor dust and solar radiation will have on my plants. They are in a delicate phase of pollination. I shouldn't even be here, but Tom wanted to come and Kasandra insisted. We should swing by after the party. This is a critical stage." Erica brushed the curls, which cascaded around her face and long neck, back over her shoulder.

"Well, you both clean up lovely." Teddy hoped to change the subject from Erica's plants. Once she got started, it seemed to be all she ever talked about.

"We're all smartly dress including the lovely doctor. I'm sorry Sally couldn't be here tonight." Erica winked obviously enough for everyone to see, including the sheriff.

"She's in New York for a conference—"

There were chimes that cut off conversation and everyone quieted down. Kasandra's voice rang through the rooms of the house like a disembodied spirit. "Good evening, everyone. If you all want to make your way out to the patio, I believe we are getting the first signs that the meteor shower is readying to start."

Slowly everyone began to pile out the doors into the backyard. There was enough light so that people could see, but Kasandra had everything dimmed so that the illuminations in the sky wouldn't be hindered. Seeing the continued flashes of blue and purple, Teddy didn't think that would be an issue.

Teddy stood with the doc and the sheriff as Casey quickly joined them.

"There you are." She slid an arm through his. "Isn't this amazing?"

Teddy nodded. He had to admit the sky was beautiful, and the flashes that were starting to blaze across the sky were incredible. He glanced around the crowd, trying to find Nick, but they must be on the backside of the pool house or by the fairway.

Maybe I should look for him.

Everyone continued staring up at the sky, but for Teddy, something wasn't right; the air had changed somehow. It suddenly felt charged, and he could almost taste the ozone in his mouth. Sparks started to dance on the ground. The hair on the back of his neck and his arms were on end.

"I think we need to get—"

The first strike of lightning came fast and furious; the electrical charges grew larger and ground lightning hit the pool, then another bolt of energy crossed the horizon. Soon there were strikes all over the backyard and on the golf course. Teddy grabbed Casey and the two made it back into the house just as a lightning bolt hit the tree next to the pool house. The screams echoed throughout as everyone rushed back into the house for shelter. The lights flicked and started to explode around the room.

"Nick? Where's Nick?" There was another explosion and Casey grabbed his arm.

Outside in the backyard, additional bolts of energy hit the gardens and one hit the chimney of the pool house with a loud explosion.

"Oh, God," Casey yelled. "The station. The radio tower."

"Nicky!" Teddy called out, scanning the rooms in all the confusion.

Tom was next to Casey as the light behind him and Erica popped. "WLKV has an automated emergency broadcast, right?"

Casey nodded and ducked, as an overhead light exploded. Teddy pulled her and the sheriff away from the sparks. "Of course. We updated it a few months back."

"Then it'll get the word out." Tom pulled Erica close to him as another loud popping sound came from the lights in the house and then made its way outside.

"We got everyone in the house." Doc rushed over, pulling off his jacket.

"What about Nick?" Teddy grabbed his arm.

"I think, we got everyone from the pool house," Doc said. "Was that supposed to happen? Why didn't they warn us?"

"No." Erica shook her head. The curls around her face frizzed out with the electricity in the air. "There must have been too much of a charge in the atmosphere. This shouldn't last long. I hope."

As quickly as it started, the electrical strikes stopped, but the house was cast in darkness, filled only by the eerie blue and purple glow of the night sky. Mumbles broke out as everyone looked for friends and family.

"Nick?" Teddy grabbed Casey's hand. "Where's Nick?" He checked the room for his son. People were standing around, others were sitting, but he didn't see Nick. Off with her mother, Teddy saw Jenny with some of the other kids. Thank God they got them out of the pool house. He waved to Jenny and she waved back. She pulled on her mother's hand and made her way over to Teddy.

"Mr. Teddy. Mr. Teddy," she screamed and rushed into his arms.

"Jenny. Sweetness, you okay?"

"We're fine." Jacqueline pushed the fallen strands of hair out of her face. "Just terrified. I've never seen anything like that in my life. Mark went to make sure no one is in the pool house."

"Nick went off with some of the older boys." Jenny pulled at her dress. "They told me not to tell, but I'm scared he's hurt. We've got to find him. He's always so nice to me."

"Fuck," Teddy said, not bothering to censor his language. "I bet they went to the greenhouse to drink."

"Don't be mad at him." Jenny raised her voice, surprising Teddy. "He's only nice to those boys because ..." Her face dropped and she kicked at the floor.

Teddy knelt down and raised her chin with his hand. "What is it, Jenny? You can tell me."

"He's only nice to them so they won't make fun of you." She frowned, her voice barely a whisper. "They call you awful names. They're mean. I heard them making fun of him and you, but instead of fighting with them, Nick told them he could get them beer and stuff. He made me promise not to tell. So, don't be mean to him, please?"

Teddy bit as his lip. "It's okay, Sweetness. Thank you for telling me." He glanced over his shoulder at Casey and Doc.

Kasandra rushed over to the group. "Sheriff, it's Lisa." She handed him the phone.

Teddy stood up.

"At least the phones work." Doc nodded. "Let's start checking if anyone's hurt," he said to Casey.

"Doc, I need to get to the station. People are going to need information. I can't just stay here. I have a responsibility to this town." Casey made for the door.

"And I need to get to the hospital. I'll take you to the station on my way. Let's just make sure everyone here is okay first."

Casey nodded.

The doc took her hand and pulled Jenny and Jacqueline toward the other groups standing around the house.

"Lisa, what's the sitrep?" Tom spoke quietly, and their small group listened on as they all waited for him to speak. Finally, after what felt like hours to Teddy, Tom finally spoke. "Okay, call county fire and get them over to Erica's lab and greenhouse. My ETA is ten minutes. I want you and Greg out patrolling town. Tell folks to stay inside, use the PA system on the cruisers. I'm sure Lakeview Power is already working on the power, but who knows how long it'll be out." Tom faced Teddy. "Lisa, Teddy's son is missing. We think he's at the greenhouse with some friends. If you see them, call me. We're heading out now." He hung up the phone.

"Teddy, you can come if you want, but why don't you stay here in case Nick and friends make it back this way? If we find him, we'll call you."

Teddy nodded.

"Honey, you can stay here as long as you need. Why don't we get folks to help us look for the boys? We can head slowly in the direction of the greenhouse. I swear I never thought they would sneak off."

"Erica, do you think the worst is over?" Tom asked.

"I'm not an astrophysicist, but I think so."

Tom nodded. "Be safe everyone, and if you see it start to spark up, head for cover quick."

"Thanks, Sheriff." Teddy nodded. "I hope Nick's okay, that little shit. I hope he's all right so I can kick his butt."

•   •   •

Teddy paced back and forth. The bright white tile and the boring white walls only reminded him how much he hated hospitals. What the hell is up with that generic landscape? He walked over and straightened it. Then there was the antiseptic smell. It turned his stomach. It had been hours and nothing. What was taking the doc so long?

There only seemed to be minor damage around town. Except for the fire at the lab and greenhouse. Which was good for the town, but not for Erica. He couldn't imagine how she was going to react. Power was still out, but the hospital was on its emergency generator and everyone was running around dealing with the injured. So he waited here out of the way.

The doors opened, and Teddy found his thumbnail in his mouth. "Doc," Teddy said. Walking in next to him was Nicky.

"Oh Nicky, baby boy." Teddy rushed and hugged him. "How is he?" He ran hands through Nick's hair and examined him for injuries. His shirt was dirty and his tie was MIA, but otherwise he seemed fine.

"He's all good," Doc patted his shoulder. "Just needed some oxygen to help clear out his lungs of the smoke."

"Oh God." Teddy pulled away from Nick and stared at the doctor.

"Dad, I'm fine." Nick coughed.

"You can take him home. I gave him an inhaler just in case he needs it, but I think he'll be fine." Doc wiped his brow clean of the sweat.

Teddy gave Doc a big hug. "Thank you."

Doc laughed. "That's what I do. Now if you'll excuse me, I have others to check on."

Teddy nodded.

Nick grunted, "Thanks, Doc."

"Be careful getting home," Doc said and walked out the waiting room.

Teddy pulled Nick over to the beige sofa and sat him down. "We need to talk."

"Now?" Nick rested his suit jacket on his legs.

"I don't want you hanging out with those boys anymore." Teddy raised a hand to cut off Nick protest. "I know you only hang out with them to protect me, but I'm fine. Let them do or say whatever they want about me. I can take it. I've been taking it my whole life. You don't need to be my defender."

Nick glanced down at the floor. "I don't even like them."

"Then fuck 'em." Teddy lifted Nick's face so he could talk to him, man to man. "Nicky, you're my world, and tonight you being gone scared me more than anything. I know I'm not your real dad, but I would do anything for you. Don't let people like them turn you into someone you're not. You're a good boy. You're turning into an amazing young man."

"Thanks, Papabear." Nicky reached over and hugged Teddy. "Am I still grounded?"

"So grounded." Teddy chuckled as he hugged him back.

•　　　•　　　•

"Enough!" Teddy shouted from the kitchen island. Nick had been out of the hospital for two days, and he was acting insane. "You almost got killed and now you're talking crazy. There is nothing wrong with anyone in town, Nick."

"I didn't almost get killed. It was just smoke from the fire." Nick crossed his arms over his chest. "How can you not see it? Ever since the meteor shower, some people just don't seem right." He raked a hand through his hair. "Have you seen Dr. Phuong and the sheriff? You can't tell me there is nothing wrong with them. What about Dee at the diner?"

"This is ridiculous." Teddy rubbed his temples.

The kitchen in his home was simple. It was a big room with all the appliances and cabinets on one wall and a huge work island in the middle. On the opposite side of the room was a table with four chairs. He really wanted to update it, get rid of the chicken wallpaper his mother put up a million years ago, but he never seemed to have time.

"So, it's normal for Dr. Phuong to strut around town dressed like a hooker? And flirt with anything that moves. I tried to apologize for all the trouble we caused her and she told me that it was fine. We were just being boys, but Dad, I'm telling you she was vacant. There was nothing there. She was cold as ice. It was creepy. And what about the sheriff? Is it normal to quarantine the area around the greenhouse and Dr. Phuong's lab? And why all of a sudden are people who don't normally work at CAGE there at all hours? Why is Jenny's mother there? What are they doing there?"

Teddy crossed his arms over his chest. "They are probably helping Dr. Phuong get settled. Her lab was destroyed—"

"And CAGE Manufacturing, a paper manufacturer, is set up for a biologist?" Nick shook his head. "That makes no sense."

"I don't know, maybe? Why does it matter? And what are you doing lurking around CAGE?"

"I followed the Mayor and Jenny's mom there yesterday. What does it matter? Especially if everything is all right? I didn't do anything."

"You did what?" Teddy reached up and started massaging his temples. "Jesus, Nick. I can't even. Listen, you need to cut this crap out. If something happens to CAGE and they think it was you, you'll end up in jail or worse." Teddy took a breath and tried to calm his breathing and his pounding heart. He quickly glanced to the bottle of pills by the sink. "Look, if you kids weren't responsible for the fire at the greenhouse—"

"That wasn't us. One of the meteors hit the building and everything caught fire." Nick grabbed his book bag. "We hadn't even gotten there yet when all hell broke loose. You should have smelled it, Dad. It was awful, like burning flesh."

With shaky hands, Teddy put a sandwich and a small bag of chips in the brown bag and pushed it toward Nick. "You know, you're lucky Tom doesn't arrest you. He's waiting for the fire investigators to come from Kansas City to find out what really happened. If it was the meteors, then you have nothing to worry about."

"We know what happened," Nick's voice raised as did the color in his face. "It was a meteor. They hit all over town. Remember? Why is it only the lab and greenhouse are quarantined and not Ms. St. Martin's home or the Feed and Seed downtown or any of the other places the meteors hit?"

"Because Dr. Phuong's was a lab and there might be chemicals or something, and Tom doesn't believe it was just a meteor. He thinks that those dumbass kids you hung out with were into something else," Teddy said.

"It wasn't us. It's them. They're hiding something, and now they're using CAGE to cover it up."

"Who them? The sheriff? Erica? The mayor? Jenny's mother? The fire chief? The volunteer firefighters? The people at CAGE? Who is them, Nick?"

"I don't know. Maybe all of them. They were all there." Nick ran a hand through his hair. "What if something in the meteor storm affected the plants or her experiments?

What if the fire affected people and turned them into something? What if now they are trying to turn more people? What happens when the people from Kansas City get here? What if—"

"Stop!" Teddy banged his hand on the counter. "Now you listen to me. You're going to school. You're coming straight to the shop afterward and doing your homework. Once I close the salon, we're coming home and you're going to your room. Do you understand me?"

Nick's gaze blazed like his father's. It was full of rage, but this time directed right at Teddy.

"I said, do you understand?"

"F-fine!" Nick rushed out the kitchen door, and it slammed behind him.

"What am I going to do?" Teddy mumbled as he walked to the sink, barely able to hold the glass with water in his shaking hands.

•   •   •

The door jingled as Casey strolled into Teddy's shop. Her hair was pulled back into a ponytail. Her KC sweatshirt had the sleeves pushed up. She took a seat on the purple sofa.

"They're crazy?"

"Who?" Teddy put down the broom and checked his book. His next appointment wasn't for an hour, assuming he showed up.

A lot of folks have canceled the past couple of days. Probably still freaked out by the meteor storm.

"The sheriff." Casey dusted off her jeans. "Since the meteor shower—I know it's only been four days—but he's been riding my butt about the radio station and how I need to take everything off-line so it can be inspected. If I do that, the town won't have anything. We'll be cut off from the rest of the world. Have you noticed the phones are hit and miss?"

Teddy narrowed his eyes. "I haven't had any issues with the phones."

"Try calling out of our area. Try calling Kansas City or Des Moines. It's almost impossible." Casey huffed. "Anyway, today, I got a visit from the fire chief. I can't believe Tom sicced the chief on me. Now I have the two of them all up in my business. The downtime is going to kill me financially." She sighed. "What a pain."

Teddy frowned, tugging at his shirt to fan himself. "Does he seem different to you?"

"Who?" Casey leaned back and stretched her arms on the back of the sofa.

"Tom, the sheriff." Teddy crossed over and sat on the couch next to her.

"You mean other than being a pain in the ass? No. I don't think so." She shook her head. "He's always been kind of odd. I suppose it's the military background of his. But, well, he has a lot to deal with right now. They are still trying to sort out what happened at the lab and greenhouse. And poor Erica."

"About that." Teddy glanced out the big picture window. Why was he suddenly feeling like they were trapped here? *Ridiculous.* "Why did they move her over to CAGE? Seems kind of odd a botanist would be working out of a paper manufacturer."

Casey shrugged.

"I heard Frank wasn't happy that he had to give up some of his warehouse space the other day. Lisa said he was in yelling at the sheriff, but this morning when I saw him at the diner, I mentioned that I was sorry about the loss of space at CAGE, but that it was real nice of him, and he didn't seem to care. He said he didn't need all that space."

"You know Frank's a hothead." Casey sighed. "Once he blew up at the sheriff, it was probably out of his system."

"I suppose, but ...but he seemed to be a vacant kind of lost. It was like he said the words but there was nothing behind them. Kind of like a doll or something."

Casey's brows rose as she watched him. "I think you've taken one too many of your anxiety pills."

Teddy frowned. "What about Erica? Isn't it odd that she's acting the way she is? I didn't even think she had those kinds of clothes and all that makeup."

"She kind of looks like she ransacked Kasandra's closet." Casey laughed.

Teddy crossed his arms over his chest.

Casey's smile vanished from her face. "Doc said it's the stress of losing all her work and research. She promised to go and talk to him. So, she's getting help. Maybe he'll put her on something."

"I suppose. It just seems a little odd."

"How would you feel if you lost your shop, or Nick? It's kind of like that for her. At least she's got the Sheriff."

"I guess you're right. I was really upset when Nick went missing."

"Teddy, everyone's been through a lot this week. I'm sure people are all shell-shocked. Honestly, it's nice to see the folks at CAGE helping Erica out."

•   •   •

Teddy watched as Nick focused on his breakfast, stirring the eggs from one side of the plate to the other. He had been more and more despondent over the last couple of days. His school uniform hung from him; even its messy nature had no life to it.

"Anything special happening at school today?" Teddy cautiously took a bite of his toast. Conversation these past few days with Nick was the equivalent of walking through a field full of landmines.

"No." Nick continued to play with the eggs on his plate.

"Aren't you hungry?" Teddy bit his tongue, regretting the question the moment it came out. He was ready to duck under the table and wait for the boom.

"Not really." Nick put the fork down.

This can't be good. Time to change tactics.

"I was thinking, if you want, tonight, we could see a movie. You know some guy time." Teddy tried smiling, but Nick wasn't facing him. "With everything back to normal, it might be a nice break." He reached out for Nick's hand, but he pulled it away. "You can pick."

"Whatever." Nick shrugged.

"Nicky, what's wrong?" Teddy reached for his hand again, but Nick moved farther away.

"Nothing." Nick wiped at his eyes. "According to you and everyone else." Nick's tone was sour, and he still wasn't facing Teddy, only his dish of scrambled eggs.

Teddy bit his upper lip.

What am I supposed to do?

"Nick, come on. Talk to me?"

Nick finally met Teddy's gaze. His eyes had dark circles under them and the whites of his eyes were bloodshot.

"Have you been sleeping? Are you sick? What's wrong?"

"It doesn't matter. You won't believe me. I told you something is wrong with the sheriff and Erica and now ..." He shook his head. "It doesn't matter."

Teddy's heart dropped. Something was affecting his son, his complexion and coloring were awful. Of course, he wasn't sleeping. "Yes, it matters. I love you and I'm worried about you. I want to help."

"Then let's leave," Nick said. "We could go today. We could take Ms. St. Martin. And Jenny. I think she's still okay, but not her parents." He shook his head. There was actual hope in Nick's voice and his eyes. "We could get the hell out of this place. I don't even care where we go."

"Nick, I can't up and leave. I've got clients. You have school. This is our home, and I know Jenny's parents. We sure can't take her with us. And Kasandra, well, she would be up for anything probably, but no." The words dropped from Teddy's mouth and he hated saying them, but it was the truth. When you're an adult, you can't just drop everything and go on a trip.

Life doesn't work that way.

"Why not? It's not like we're trapped in some cage." Nick's shoulders dropped, and he sank deeper into the kitchen chair.

Not trapped, but I have responsibilities. Maybe it's the same thing to him.

"Look, why don't we go away for the holiday?" Teddy didn't want to give up. Maybe this was the *in* he needed to reach Nick. "We could go anywhere you want. You name the place and we'll go."

"It's so far away, by then it'll be too late. There won't be anyone left and ..." Nick's voice faded as he spoke.

"Don't say that. It's not too late. We'll have a blast." Teddy tried to sound excited, but this wasn't his son. At this point, he would take the smart-ass troublemaker compared to this.

"I have to get to school." Nick stood up and grabbed his backpack and lunch from the counter. He walked over to where his coat was hung and knocked his and Teddy's jackets off the hook. "You love me, right, Dad?" Nick hung Teddy's jacket back up and put his coat on slipping his hands into his pockets.

"Of course I love you. You're my little Nickers." Teddy rushed over to Nick and hugged him. He squeezed him as tight as he could, and to his surprise, Nick gave him a tight hug in return. "Tonight, movie night, I promise."

"Okay." Nick detached himself from Teddy's hug and headed out the door.

Teddy waited for Nick to cross the street, then hurried to the phone. He dialed and waited, clicking his nails together.

"Dr. Hudson," Doc's voice said on the other end of the line.

"Doc, thank goodness," Teddy gasped as he leaned against the counter.

"Teddy, is everything alright?"

"I don't know." Teddy shook his head. "Nick doesn't seem himself. He's so depressed and I'm worried. He says something wrong here in town, but I don't know. Could it be a side effect of what happened the night of the meteor shower? What about a virus?"

"Maybe. Why don't you bring him in and we can have a conversation? I'll give him an exam too."

"You don't think something's wrong with him, do you?"

"Honestly." Doc lowered his voice. "Teddy, I don't know, but he's not the only one to say there's something wrong with the town or at least some people in town. It could be an after effect of the smoke from the fire and the meteor shower, but I'm not sure."

"Should I pull him from school? What if it's a virus or some kind of outbreak? Will you need to seal off the town?" Teddy fanned his face.

"Teddy, don't get yourself worked up. Do you have your anxiety medicine?"

"Yes."

"Have you taken any today?"

"No."

"I suggest you take one." Doc took a breath. "Everything will be fine. People are probably still dealing with stress or anxiety over what happened. As for Nick, it had to scare him to see the lab and greenhouse go up like that, as well as being out in the lightning strikes. That had to be terrifying."

Teddy nodded. Hearing Doc's words calmed his nerves.

"Can you bring him around noon today?" Doc asked.

"I'll make it work. Thanks, Doc."

"See you and Nick later." The phone hung up.

Teddy stood at the counter and a nervous chuckle escaped his lips. He hadn't realized that his heart was pounding in his chest till that moment. He glanced out the window at the yard, with the houses and the town just beyond. The sky was blue and a few clouds drifted by on this picture-perfect early November day.

"Everything is fine. Nicky is fine." He reached for his pills and quickly popped one in his mouth, then dry swallowed it.

Teddy cleared the plates from the table and put everything in the dishwasher, ensuring that breakfast was cleaned up and put away. Satisfied with the way the kitchen looked, he grabbed his jacket and checked for his car keys.

"Don't tell me I misplaced my keys. Dammit! I could have sworn they were in my jacket last night."

•   •   •

Lisa burst through his salon doors. "Teddy!" Her hair was a mess. Her bright green eyes burned into him. She was panting and sweating.

"Jesus, Lisa." Teddy stepped back from his client and put the scissors on his workstation. "I almost cut off Ms. Maribel's ear."

The older woman glanced over at him.

"I didn't. You're fine." He patted her shoulder.

"Is everything all right, dear?" Ms. Maribel asked.

"Hello, Ms. Maribel." Lisa nodded at her. "Teddy, you need to listen to me and we have to go." Lisa rushed over to Teddy and took his arm.

"What on earth are you talking about?" Teddy glanced over at the clock. It was eleven in the morning. He had forty-five minutes before he needed to pick up Nick and get to the hospital.

Thank goodness Casey's letting me use her truck today. Especially since she and Kasandra were spending the day together.

"It's Nick," she said. "He's got your car. The sheriff and Greg are following him, but he's on his way to CAGE, we think."

"Oh God," Teddy said and started for the door.

His shop filled with a flash of white light, followed by an explosion that rattled the entire building and broke the large picture windows of his shop.

Teddy rushed back to protect Ms. Maribel. Lisa did her best to protect the two of them but landed on the floor next to the chair.

"What the hell was that?" Teddy shouted, his ears ringing.

"Lisa, come in. Lisa, are you there?" her walkie-talkie squealed with Greg's voice.

Teddy was helping Ms. Maribel, making sure she was all right.

"What the hell happened?" Lisa shouted, dusting off the glass and giving Teddy a hand with Ms. Maribel.

Teddy stared out what used to be the window. People filled the street, cars stopped in their place right in the middle of the Main Street. Everyone was pointing and looking in the direction of CAGE Manufacturing. Some people had blank empty looks like Dee and Bill, others filled with panic and terror.

"Nick he ...oh God, we think he killed Erica with the car. Maybe the sheriff ... started a fire at CAGE. Do you have Teddy? I think Nick's heading to the country club. He's got Jenny."

6

The present.

"No." TEDDY WEPT, getting out of his car. He tried to take a step on the path that led to Kasandra's home. "I don't want to relive this. It's not what happen. Nick would never have done that. Never. He was just sick then. He got better."

Teddy fumbled and reached for his pills, but the bottle was gone. It must have fallen out of his pocket, still in the car. He took a deep breath; he could do this. They would be there soon. He walked the rest of the way to what remained of the front door of Kasandra's home. There was a flash of lightning, followed by a loud bang as Kasandra's body dropped to the floor in a spray of blood. Teddy didn't know where to look, but he didn't want to see this. An explosion blew out from the sliding wall of glass doors. He closed his eyes tight, but Casey and Jenny both lay in puddles of blood and gore, glass shards around them. Nick's scream pierced Teddy's ears and forced his eyes open.

"The Doc is dead," Greg yelled, sweat pouring from his brow. "Fucking Nick shot him at CAGE! Got the sheriff's gun. What the hell is happening here? Why were all those people looking all blank like that? Lisa, what the fuck is happening to this town?" Greg forced out a breath.

Teddy caught Greg's focus. He was narrowing on Nick. Teddy saw the gun in Greg's hand slowly start to rise. Teddy pushed Greg at the last second and the shot missed its intended target and hit Lisa. The right side of her lovely face vanished in a spray of blood and flesh.

"No!" Nick yelled—or was it Teddy?

Another flash of lightning and pop of thunder and Greg hit the ground next to Teddy, the back of his head gone, offering a clear view of the polished tile beneath. Teddy bent down and pulled the gun from Greg's lifeless hand.

"You didn't believe me!" Nick shouted, the gun shaking in his hand. A cut in his forehead dribbled with blood. "Now they're all gone. I tried to save them, but ..." He pointed to Kasandra's body. "That wasn't Ms. St. Martin. Not anymore. She tried to get Jenny. I had to stop her. I had to stop them. Why didn't you believe me? We could've stopped Erica and the sheriff before all this happened."

The gun rose in shaky hands. Teddy met Nicky's darkened eyes.

A blinding light filled the grand entry hall in Kasandra's home.

"I don't want to see that. I can't." Teddy pushed the images away and wiped at his eyes. He glanced back in the direction of his Mustang where his pills had to be. He inhaled, closed his eyes, and in as strong a voice as he could muster spoke. "That isn't what happened. None of that is real. He was a baby. My baby! He would never do that. He couldn't. They wouldn't be coming today if that happened."

Teddy ran a hand along the rough edges of the crumbling doorjamb of Kasandra's house. He focused on the present. His friends and his son.

Thunder rumbled. He peeked over his shoulder and beamed. All the awful visions melted away.

"You found me." He stepped away from the door and the collapsing porch, quickly swiping away the dampness of his eyes.

"Of course I did." Nick's face filled with a bright smile. "You silly old man."

"Still young enough to kick your sorry ass, little boy!" Teddy chuckled.

"I've missed you, Papabear." He wrapped his arms around Teddy.

The image of the little boy running up to him after school, beaming up at him, filled Teddy's mind and warmed his heart.

Nick had grown exactly into what he had imagined he would, a handsome man with broad shoulders and a dimpled chin. Just like his jerk of a father. *The louse. Only good thing I got from him was Nick.* It was no wonder that Jenny said yes so quickly when Nick proposed. The youngest of their group were now all grown up as they should be, Nick was thirty-six and Jenny thirty.

"Have you seen the others?" Teddy stepped back from his son.

"Not yet," Nick replied. "But I'm sure they're on their way."

Nick and Teddy silently made their way back to the Mustang. He loved these few moments with Nick, just the two of them.

"How about a quick go around the block?" Nick grinned, a twinkle in his eyes.

"No way." Teddy nudged him.

They fell silent. What had been said today was the same thing that would be said tomorrow and a year from now. There was a distant flash of lightning and a hollow rumble of thunder.

"You just had to be first, didn't you?" Doc stepped out of the mist.

The sky grew darker, but Teddy warmed from head to toe at hearing Doc's voice. Teddy turned.

Doc pulled his hat tighter around his gray hair. A clap of thunder from the approaching storm drew his attention to the sky. He pointed to Teddy's Mustang. "You kept your little toy."

"Of course! What did you expect?" Teddy flourished with his hand. "It's fabulous like me."

Doc lowered his head, trying to hide his smile.

"It's nice to see you again, Doc." Nick offered his hand.

Another rumble of thunder caught the three men's attention.

Lisa and Greg approached out of the shadows opposite from Doc.

"You're double-parked." Greg's eyes were narrow and his lips pulled tight. "I could give you a ticket." His scowl turned into a smile.

"I don't think you have that kind of power anymore, but nice try, Deputy Dipshit." Teddy winked.

"Whatever, Teddy." Greg rubbed his mouth to stifle a chuckle. He still had his typical stubble, most of it gray.

"Hey, girly-girl." Teddy hugged Lisa. She felt so cold even through her thick jacket. The coming storm would only make things colder.

They all must be freezing.

"Hey, Teddy." Lisa returned the hug.

They are all getting so old, but that's to be expected with time. Her bright green eyes are dulled with age.

Greg jerked his thumb toward the dilapidated house. "Looks like shit, doesn't it?"

"We'll see how good you look after twenty years of no one taking care of you." Lisa crossed over to Nick, giving him a hug and a kiss on the cheek.

The corners of Teddy's mouth curled up into a grin at their banter.

Lisa glanced around at the landscape, then crossed her arms over her ample chest. "Hard to believe that today is twenty years."

"Time flies when you're having fun." Doc rubbed his hands together, blowing into them.

Greg scoffed, sticking out his hand in greeting to Doc. "You call this fun, Doc? Being out like this, coming to a town that's dead as shit?" They shook hands. "Can't even get a drink."

Teddy remembered that last night before the meteor-shower viewing party. Greg nursed his beer, complaining about the coming meteor shower and having to work while Doc reminded him it was nothing to worry about. How wrong they all had been.

"Or sing karaoke?" Lisa smirked, giving Doc a peck on the cheek. She stepped back to Greg, grinning at him.

"Love Shack" is forever ruined for me, thanks to Greg.

Doc shrugged. "It is what it is."

Another boom of thunder caught their attention.

"Indeed," Tom said as he and Erica came into view. The darkness of the shadows released them as they neared the group.

"Nice of you two to join us, Sheriff." Lisa frowned, glancing between the both of them.

"Sorry, we were detained." Tom adjusted his utility belt. His hand moved to where his gun would normally be. He frowned.

You're not going to need it. Not anymore. It's all over.

"I'm sure you were." Greg ran a hand over his chin.

Tom tightened his lips to a thin line.

Erica gave Doc a wink. "Good to see ya, Doc. You look good as always."

If Erica hadn't ended up with Tom, she would have probably made a play for Doc. He would have never done anything; he was too in love with his wife. Of course, when things started to happen, people changed, so it was possible it could have been Erica and Doc standing here together with Tom off to the side.

"Lovely as always, Erica. My wife would be jealous that you never change." Doc nodded to her, then buttoned the last button on his coat. He faced Nick, his eyes narrowing. "I see the scar healed."

"Finally," Nick said. "A distant memory, much like the accident."

The accident that put us all on this path. Teddy reached out and brushed the hair away from Nick's eyes. *He's still my baby boy.*

"I wish I could've taken a look at it." Doc stepped closer to Nick for a quick inspection. "We might have minimized the scarring."

"It's a good reminder," Greg said. "For what he—"

"Be nice," Lisa interrupted.

Greg sighed.

"You weren't in the best of shape at the time, Doc." Nick absently rubbed his forehead where the scar was.

Teddy was glad Nick ignored the remark. He was only a boy and couldn't be held responsible for his actions.

"Would've been nice if you were on time," Greg grumbled and pointed to the sky. "This isn't gonna get any better."

Same old Greg, can't let it go.

"Serious, Greg, lighten up. It could be worse." Erica fixed her light-green scarf.

"Really? How—?"

"Come on, guys," Teddy interrupted Greg. "Behave. We don't get a lot of time together. Let's not fight."

"Anyway," Erica started, "I had to stop and investigate my plants at the old greenhouse. This is the only time I get to see them."

Those cursed plants. Whatever those meteors did to them, I hope they've finally died. They made everyone crazy.

Teddy took a breath. *Let it go. It's over. It doesn't matter and everyone is here, nice and safe just like I knew they would be.*

Erica tucked her arm through Tom's, pulling him a bit closer. "We could hardly find them. Nature is taking everything back. In another hundred years, almost all trace of mankind will be erased from this place and my plants will be fully incorporated into the ecosystem. But they won't be the same."

"Good." Greg crossed his arms.

"Be nice." Lisa glared at him. "I can make your life hell."

"Who's still missing?" Teddy's voice called all their attention back. He counted his friends, but the growing shadows and the angry gray sky made it harder to see.

"Kasandra, Casey, and Jenny." Nick looked around the group.

"And why didn't Jenny come with you?" Erica snuggled closer to Tom.

Nick's gaze dropped to the ground as he kicked at a small stone.

"Next time, I'll have Lisa come with them," Greg said. "Heck, maybe even Erica, so they can all be late together." He laughed. "Women, am I right?"

Lisa punched him in the arm, and Erica glared at him.

Greg winced and rubbed the spot. "Truth hurts," he said, this time sidestepping Lisa to dodge the second punch.

"For you." Lisa stood taller. "I don't know why I ever married you?"

"Because I'm sexy as hell." Greg flexed his arms. "And amazing in bed."

There were groans all around.

"What?" Greg smirked with a shrug of his shoulder. "It's true."

Lisa wiggled her pinky finger and laughed, joined by Erica.

It was good to hear laughter in this dark place. It was so much like the days before the disaster that brought them all here. Everyone, especially these people, laughed a lot. It was why Teddy loved them all. Especially back then. He could count on that laughter to brighten his mood and his spirits. They always had a way to lessen his anxiety. Those were brighter days. Days filled with light. Not like now.

Why is that?

Lightning flashed in the distance, followed by more thunder.

Nick pulled his jacket tighter.

"If they don't get here soon, we're all gonna get wet ... and not the good kind of wet." Teddy waggled his eyebrows.

"Water won't kill ..." Nick paused and his gaze fell again.

Teddy reached out and lifted his son's chin, then nudged his cheek. Nick's face brightened.

"Whose bright idea was this again?" Casey's bubbly voice called out to the group as she bounced up the path. "Someone didn't listen to my weather report."

"You haven't had a weather report in years." Tom rested his hand on his utility belt.

Casey scowled at him.

Greg, Doc, and Teddy all chuckled.

"Anyway. Who do we have to blame for this?" Casey said. Jenny was by her side, seemingly trying to keep to Casey's shadow.

"Me, bitch, so get over it and give me some sugar." Teddy pointed to the empty spot in front of him.

"Good to see you, Teddybear." Casey jumped into his arms, hugging him. "Sorry we're late. You know how it is."

"And there's my little girl." Teddy waved. "Come here, sweetness." He reached out for Jenny, pulling her from behind Casey.

Jenny had grown into the beautiful woman he imagined she would. She was still petite, but with amazing curves and beautiful blonde hair.

Teddy grabbed Nick's hand and put it in Jenny's, pushing them to stand next to each other. "That's better, just the way it should be."

Nick leaned in, kissed her forehead, and they embraced.

The others chitchatted, getting reacquainted as Teddy studied Nick and Jenny. He loved seeing them together. They would always be little kids that needed protecting. Nick, the abused son of his jerk of a biological father, and Jenny, left to wander by his salon and spend hours sitting and watching him cut hair. She would drink a pop or nibble on some chips. They were the ones he'd looked forward to seeing most. They were the truly innocent ones. Things should have never involved them, but it wasn't like there were options. It all happened, and they got swept away in the events like everyone else.

"Are you taking care of my son, Sweetness?" Teddy finally asked Jenny, sensing the lull in the conversation. He fussed with her raincoat and scarf, ensuring she was protected from the chill in the air.

"I'm doing my best, but Nick can be a handful. I don't think he ever grew out of his teen escapades."

"Hey." Nick glared at her. "It was just one joyride—"

"In my car." Teddy frowned at him. "Without a license." Teddy crossed his arms over his chest.

Erica turned to Nick and her eyes narrowed. "What a mess that ride of yours turned out to be, especially for

Tom and I, not to mention poor Doc."

Teddy nodded, a pang of guilt making his heart skip. *If I'd kept better track of my keys, but he would have gotten them anyway. He was so determined.* There was another flash of lightning and a clap of thunder as rain started to fall in the distance over the lake.

No. It's too soon.

"I hope Miss Thing gets here." Teddy shrugged his jacket tighter. "This is ridiculous, even for her."

"Did someone call?" Kasandra burst from the shadows onto the scene, her arms wide as she made a grand entrance. She pranced down the crumbling pathway like it was one of those Paris runways she always bragged about.

Teddy chuckled as the others shook their heads.

"Ever the diva." Doc tapped his watch.

"Like you'd want me any other way, Doc." Kasandra kissed both his cheeks. "Sorry I'm late, everyone. You know how it is." Kasandra greeted everyone else with air kisses.

"It's nice to see you all." Teddy glanced around. Every year at this time, he experienced the warmth and the love of friendship as well as the cold and the sorrow of loss. "Too bad we can't do this more often."

"Given the state of things, it looks like there won't be much more reason to come. The town is all but gone." Doc pointed to Kasandra's house. One of the few remaining walls blew over with a stiff gust of wind from the storm, as if to emphasize his point.

"I should have sued the builders." Kasandra frowned as she examined her fingernails. "I spent so much money on that place, and for it to be in this state after only twenty years ..." She crossed her arms.

"It wasn't their fault," Erica said. "After what happened and CAGE burning, there was no one around to care for it. No building, no matter how well constructed, could have withstood that. We can't control time or Mother Nature."

"I'll give you this." Tom craned his neck to view the remains of the house. "In its day, that house was beautiful."

"I blame crappy construction." Greg kicked at the broken brick path.

"And none of that is Kasandra's fault." Lisa adjusted her jacket.

"It doesn't matter anyway," Tom said. "At last count, there were only five families living—"

"That was four years ago, Sheriff," Greg interrupted. "There's no one for a hundred miles now."

"Oh, wow," Tom scratched under the brim of his sheriff's hat.

Erica frowned. "What a shame. It was such a beautiful place, all the trees and the lake. It's why I moved here."

Lisa scrutinized their surroundings. "Not so much these days ..." She peeked over at Erica. "You probably like it this way? All the plants."

"I love nature, but I don't like how all the unique Victorian architecture of the town is almost gone, and I certainly don't like what caused the town to die or what almost happened to us," Erica said.

"None of us like what's happened," Nick said. "I only ..."

"It's too late for that." Casey reached out and rested a hand on Nick's shoulder.

The sky grew darker, and the first drops of rain reached them.

No. It can't be time. Each year, less and less time. Why is this happening like this?

Teddy opened his umbrella. The drops of rain grew bigger and harder and soon the members of the group slipped away without a word. First, Doc was gone with a tap and wave of the hand. Then Greg and Lisa, only offering nods before they disappeared from sight. Tom and Erica snuggled so close together, they melted into one and vanished down the path with a splash of rain. Kasandra dabbed at her eyes and tried to reach out, but she was gone. Each of their faces vanishing.

Each year with them, the time got shorter and shorter. Soon there would be no more time. Then what would happen to them?

Casey, Teddy's Casey, managed to blow him a kiss, which he caught easily and held to his cheek before she left.

He reached out for Nick and Jenny with both hands.

They each took one, gave it a squeeze, and with a flash of lightning and a splatter of rain, they were gone.

Every year, Teddy came to this spot to visit. "Goodbye," he whispered. "I'm sorry. It should have never ended the way it did. So much left unanswered. So many questions. If I would have believed Nick. If we would have left. But then Erica and Tom would have succeeded, assuming that it was still Erica and Tom." He forlornly walked through the rain, back to his Mustang. He got in. Glanced over the steering wheel.

Maybe I could've stopped this if I just listened and saw what happened around me.

Teddy turned the ignition. A blinding flash of lightning and boom of thunder filled the space outside of Kasandra's home. Teddy was gone, only a rusted Mustang remained, awkwardly parked where it had been left twenty years prior. Lakeview was empty once more.

ABOUT THE AUTHOR

M.D. Neu is an international award-winning inclusive queer Fiction Writer with a love for writing and travel. Living in the heart of Silicon Valley, and growing up around technology, he's always been fascinated with what could be. When M.D. Neu isn't writing, he works for a non-profit and travels with his biggest supporter and his harshest critic, Eric, his husband of twenty-plus years.

ALSO BY THE AUTHOR

A DRAGON FOR CHRISTMAS

M.D. Neu

Since Carmen was seven years old, she understood two things: she was going to be the strongest Dragon Keeper there ever was, and she was going to marry her best friend, Mattie.

Available in hardcover, trade paperback,
and digital editions from Water Dragon Publishing
waterdragonpublishing.com

YOU MIGHT ALSO ENJOY

ENLIGHTMENT
Bruce Golden

Forced to leave his home, a boy learns magic from a mysterious traveling old man. As time and distance takes him further from his home, the boy strives to learn everything he can from the old man before he dies.

THE JOB
Joshua Ramey-Renk

Cal Oakenflame is a mage on a mission. When Cal rescues Petra, kidnapped by sheep-stealing bandits, they uncover a plot to take over the town, led by a mysterious Preacher.

SONGS OF A DEAD FOREST
Travis Wade Beaty

A beleaguered dryad in search of safe harbor in a land ravaged by an invasive fungus finds herself at odds with a young dryad who wields the blasphemous magic of men.

Available in digital and trade paperback editions from
Water Dragon Publishing
waterdragonpublishing.com

www.ingramcontent.com/pod-product-compliance
Lightning Source LLC
Chambersburg PA
CBHW031415310726
48971CB00003B/869